Look for More Titles by Cassandra Chandler

LINGERING TOUCH

Other Works
CRAFTING A WRITER'S LIFE: Building a Foundation

Coming Soon

The Blades of Janus
PERIHELION

The Department of Homeworld Security
Nothing to Declare

Invasive Species

The Department of Homeworld Security
Book Eight

Cassandra Chandler

Copyright Page

You are a good person! You know that stealing is wrong. Remember, eBooks can't be shared or given away. It's against copyright law. So don't download books you haven't paid for or upload books in ways other people can access for free. That would be stealing.
And you're better than that.

This book is pure fiction. All characters, places, names, and events are products of the author's imagination or used solely in a fictitious manner. Any resemblance to any people, places, things, or events that have ever existed or will ever exist is entirely coincidental.

Dedication

For everyone who has dreamt of the stars.

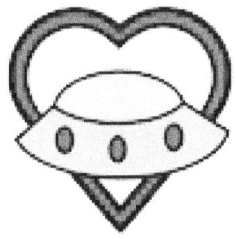

Don't miss out on any of the alien action.
Subscribe to Cassandra Chandler's newsletter at
cassandra-chandler.com!

Chapter One

"This was a mistake."

The bartender pointed at the beer in front of Kyle. "That's the drink you ordered, buddy."

"No, I was talking to myself," Kyle said.

The bartender shrugged and walked away.

"And now I really am talking to myself."

Kyle looked over at the group of friends who had insisted he join them on their trip to the bar. Supposedly, Mitch was feeling down after his most recent breakup and needed moral support. Watching him chat up every woman who passed his table made Kyle wonder if that had been a ruse. Mitch had once said, "The more beefcake in the window, the more customers stop by to shop."

Kyle picked up his drink and turned toward the mass of people dancing or playing pool or just trying to get from one place to the other in the packed room. His skin crawled.

Mitch wasn't exaggerating about Kyle's beefcake status. Navigating the thick group was going to be a pain in the ass just based on his sheer size. The messenger bag Kyle always carried would only make things worse. It wouldn't be easy to avoid bumping into people with the narrow spaces they were leaving between each other.

He watched the patterns of movement in the crowd, weaving in and out among them with only minor jostling and quite a few muttered apologies until he reached a corner that was a little quieter than the rest of the place. A couch filled the area, with a low coffee table in front of it.

Unfortunately, the couch wasn't empty. An auburn-haired woman glanced up at him from the book she was reading.

He looked at the cover—a sleek spacecraft on a star field with two familiar characters' faces superimposed in front of it all. Maybe *not* "unfortunately".

"Hi," he said.

"Hi." She smiled, her amber-brown eyes crinkling a little as if she really meant it.

He glanced around, unsure of what to say. "I don't mean to interrupt. If you're at a really good part, I can go."

"A really good part?"

He gestured toward the book. "You're going old-school. It's a special experience."

She laughed. "True. But I hate to send you back into that morass of humanity after you fought so hard to escape."

"I appreciate your compassion." As soon as he could, he would head home for some peace and quiet.

After he talked to the intriguing redhead.

"How can you read with all this noise and…chaos?" he asked.

"I have seven younger brothers and sisters. You learn."

"Wow, I can't even imagine." When she arched an eyebrow at him, he added, "Only child."

"There were days I dreamt of that. Not many, though. My siblings are cool."

He looked around at the empty seats, and said, "Are any of them here with you?"

"No, I'm with…" She looked around, then sat up a little straighter. "Hang on."

Kyle caught a glimpse of a dragon on the bookmark she tucked into her book before setting it on the table. She pulled out her phone and read something that made her let out a little snorting laugh.

"Apparently, I'm with a bunch of bailers who left an hour ago and didn't bother to tell me because 'I was busy reading'." She picked her book up again and leaned back. "If they wanted me to pay attention to them, they shouldn't have scheduled this outing on a release day."

Kyle scoffed. "I'm missing book club for this."

That same eyebrow arched on her forehead as she looked him up and down. He let out a sigh.

"No, I wasn't the High School quarterback, and yes, I do love to read. This ridiculous growth spurt," he gestured to his torso, "happened in college. It's genetic—according to my mother, who has a PhD in genetics—and it drives me crazy."

"How you must suffer from your amazing physique and movie star good looks."

He tried to ignore the sparks that crackled down his spine at her words. "Amazing, huh?"

She let out another snorting laugh. "This is a really bad pick-up ploy."

"I just wanted to get away from the crowd. When I came over here, I couldn't even see you. I wasn't trying to pick you up."

"Sure."

"But after talking to you…"

She smirked. "My mastery of sarcasm and choice in mentally stimulating pastimes has captured your interest?"

"That and your choice in authors. I set my alarm for midnight so I could wake up and read that book as soon as it downloaded."

This time, she all-out laughed. "You read Sci-fi Romance?"

"I call it 'space opera' to avoid annoying conversations. And I read everything." He waved his hand toward her book, and said, "Don't think I didn't notice that High Fantasy style dragon bookmark you're using. I know another genre-hopper when I see one."

Her eyes narrowed as she seemed to look at him for the first time. At his *face*, mostly, which was a relief.

"The only reason I'm here is because I already finished

it," he said. "I had to see how the author resolved the missing space station and find out whether Daphne and Boreal would find each other again."

"But it wasn't resolved. They found the space station, but Daphne wasn't there."

He lifted his glass. "And that is why this beverage has alcohol in it. It's going to be a long wait for the next book."

She laughed again, but the edge to it was gone. Then she scooted over on the couch to make room for him.

"Thanks." He sat next to her, and said, "I'm Kyle, by the way."

"Tracey."

He leaned forward to look at her book again. "If you're only half-way through the book, how do you know about the space station? We didn't see what happened to it till close to the end."

"Second read-through. You weren't the only one up at midnight reading a digital copy. Then I ran to my favorite bookstore as soon as it opened to get a paper version."

"That is dedication."

"Yeah. I bet you read yours on your phone at the gym."

He pulled off his bag and set it on the table, then reached inside and pulled out his pristine print copy of the book. "I was saving it to read tonight, but my friends dragged me here."

"What's that?" She pointed at the table.

His heart seemed to stutter, before it started pounding.

"That's my autoinjector."

He grabbed it, then turned it over in his hands, making sure it hadn't been damaged when it rolled out of his bag. He couldn't believe he hadn't even noticed it. There were about seven hours till he needed his next dose, but after the last time he'd been late… He never wanted to go through that agony again.

"You allergic to peanuts or something?" she said.

Kyle placed the injector back in his bag and made sure it was sealed tight. "More like the planet. Ever read H.G. Wells' *War of the Worlds?*"

"Yikes. You seem a lot nicer than those invading Martians."

"Thanks." He let the word drip with sarcasm, since it seemed to be her native language.

"On behalf of Earth, we welcome you," she said. "And your allergies. As long as you're not, you know… Trying to take over the planet."

"That isn't on my agenda for tonight." He leaned back against the couch, grinning at her as their banter put him at ease.

A super-cute bookworm who knew classic Scifi as well as modern. He might not be after the planet, but he was seriously interested in the "Earthling" in front of him. This was the most fun he'd ever had flirting. How long could they keep up the jokes about him being an alien?

'I wish,' he thought. *'It would explain a lot.'*

"Next time you're sucked into an outing on a release day, you should download the audio version," she said. "You can enjoy your book with headphones while you pretend you're at least sort of listening to the conversation."

It took him a minute to remember what they'd been talking about. When he did, he sat back, struck by how much more tolerable that would make gatherings like this in the future. "That is a great idea. I can't believe I never thought of it."

"Like I said, lots of siblings. You come up with coping mechanisms."

"When I came over here, I didn't mean to interrupt your reading. But…"

"But now that we're talking…" She leaned forward, resting her elbows on her knees. "You don't really want to stop."

"Yeah."

"Me either."

He didn't try to mask his grin as he held up his copy of the book. "I'm glad we're on the same page."

Chapter Two

Tracey slammed Kyle against the wall just to the side of the door to her apartment, devouring his mouth with hers. Okay, maybe she didn't slam him exactly, but she shoved him pretty hard, and he played along with it.

She'd untucked his shirt from his pants…maybe somewhere in the stairwell. Which was good, because she wanted to touch more of him.

His abs were rock hard—along with other parts of his anatomy. She ran her hands under his shirt, up to his chest. His pecs were just as toned.

Damn, she'd never hooked up with a guy this hot before. *And* he was a bookworm.

This might be love…

She moved her mouth to his neck, biting and sucking on his skin as she explored the arcs and valleys of his back with her fingertips. The coarse stubble on his cheeks and chin scraped against her face, along with the softer hair of his sideburns. She imagined it scraping her breasts, her stomach, the insides of her thighs…

He needed to be naked. They both did.

He grabbed a fistful of her hair and pulled her head back so he could land a crushing kiss against her mouth. His tongue stole her breath, dominating and demanding.

As he spun them around, he lifted her by her ass, pinning her to the wall a lot more effectively than she'd tried to do with him earlier. It helped that he'd lined up their hips, letting gravity settle her perfectly against him.

His dick was pressed tight to her core, making her core clench with need. She dug her fingers into his back to let out some of the tension building in her body.

He let out a little grunt as he turned his attention to her neck. Between his kisses and bites, he said, "Where are your keys?"

"In my bag. I'll get them."

He made a sound that was half growl, half moan as he let her slide down his body. Tracey turned toward the door, digging through her mini-backpack purse. The keys were barely in her hand when Kyle grabbed her hips and pulled her back against him, grinding against her ass.

She let out a moan. Her hands were shaking. Why the hell were her hands shaking? He was just a guy.

Just a smart, funny, gorgeous, amazing guy who seems as into me as I'm into him and—Oh my God, what is he doing to my neck now?

He'd started up some sort of suction action that was more stimulating than any necking she'd ever been part of. And the swirling with his tongue…

She fumbled with her keys against the lock, her fingers losing the battle to communicate with her brain as her body sent shockwaves of pleasure battering against her thought processes. His huge, strong hand in her hair, his hot lips against her neck, his dick thrusting against her, giving her a hint of what would happen as soon as the damn door would open.

Her core was already pulsing. Every little shift in her legs as he thrust against her made her tight jeans rub against her clit with delicious pressure. She wasn't sure she'd make it inside without climaxing.

"Kyle."

He tightened his grip on her hair and raked his teeth lightly against her neck. But he used his free hand to grip her shaking wrist and help steady her enough to unlock the door. She let out a breath when the mechanism clicked.

Then he dropped his hand to the front of her jeans, pressing the heel of his palm against her clit and his fingers tight to her core.

"Oh God!" She fell against the door to her apartment, sparks skittering across her vision, body alight with pleasure that exploded from everywhere.

He kept thrusting, sucking, pressing, pulling as the fireworks continued. Her neck, her core, even her scalp screamed at her to get naked now and draw this amazing man into her.

This is how he can make me feel with all our clothes

on…

Just as the climax ebbed, he turned the doorknob and opened the door. She half-fell into her apartment, but he held onto her, guiding their descent as he landed on top of her in the entryway.

Hurray for carpet.

The door slammed behind them, then his weight pressed more firmly against her. He must have kicked it shut or something.

She didn't care that her keys were still in the lock or that they were about to have sex in her foyer. She just wanted this. More of it. More of him.

He squeezed her ass, pulling her hips against his as he thrust against her.

"Too many clothes," she said.

"You get your jeans. I'll get a condom."

"Right. Condoms."

Shit. She'd been more than a little carried away. Normally, she was the one who brought up protection.

Kyle rolled off of her and yanked his messenger bag over his head. She kicked off her shoes as he started digging through it. With a frustrated grunt, he dumped it on the floor. Books and notebooks scattered across the carpet. There were little bits of paper sticking out of them and the edges were worn from use. And so many different colored pens…

Part of her had wondered if the bookworm thing was a

ruse, even after their amazing several-hours-long conversation. He looked like a jock, with his short-cropped dark hair, square jaw, and massive physique.

She really needed to give some thought to her biases. Later.

He found the box he was looking for and tore it open. She managed to keep herself from saying, "Yay!" that he had so many condoms. There were many things she wanted to do… But she'd need to get out of her jeans first.

The fastener stuck, but she managed it and the zipper. Shimmying out of them wasn't going to be the sexiest thing ever, though. He must have seen her distress, because he grabbed the waistband, peeling them down her legs for her and tossing them aside.

"Thanks, that was—" Her train of thought derailed. He'd already opened his own jeans and… "Oh, wow."

How was she going to manage that huge dick? Sure, she was more worked up than she'd ever been, but there were still limits. He was already unrolling the condom over it. Technically, that was all the clothing they needed to remove, but if he was planning to just plow into her, that would be a problem.

She could give him a blowjob while her body grew used to the idea of *that* pounding into her. The thought sent a jolt of pleasure straight to her core. She could even reach down and get herself warmed up. She'd been with guys who liked to watch that.

When she reached for him, he grabbed her by the wrists and pushed her back down, laying on top of her again. It was hot and it was sexy and it was also not happening.

"Kyle, there's no way I'm ready for you."

"I know." He raked his cheek against her neck, as if he'd noticed how much she liked his stubble in the hallway before. "But I'm way too ready for you. Just tell me if you want me to stop."

Stop what?

His dick was pressed against her thigh, not poised to get things started. He was able to grasp both of her wrists in one of his hands, freeing his other. Another jolt of not-nearly-as-pleasant energy shot through her.

"You'll let me go if I ask you to, right?" she said.

He pulled back enough to look her in the eyes. She hadn't noticed how vibrantly green his were before— almost like he was wearing colored contacts.

"I will let you go, step away, pack up my stuff, and leave right now if you want me to. Or make you pancakes in the morning if the only thing you let me do is crash on your couch so I don't have to make it home with this raging hard-on."

She laughed at the last, her tension easing. His grip loosened and he shifted farther away.

"Wait," she said. "I'm not saying I want to stop. I just didn't expect the wrist thing."

"I'm sorry. I should have asked first. The way you were

touching me…" He shook his head. "If you keep touching me like that, this isn't going to last long at all. And I want it to."

Her breath caught, her heart pounding. Of course, he only meant the sex. They'd just met. He couldn't be saying things like… Like the thoughts she wasn't letting herself think. The longing she was trying desperately to ignore.

She'd never met anyone like him before. She didn't want this to be a one-night stand.

"Kiss me, Kyle."

He lowered his weight back to her and laughed. "Gender-bending Shakespeare mashup. You are too perfect."

She couldn't believe he'd made the connection. Dammit. He was perfect, too.

Chapter Three

This was absolute bliss. Kyle had never had a lover who used her hands so much. Tracey seemed as eager to explore his skin as she was to have him slide into her. He groaned against her neck at the thought.

Not yet.

When she'd slid her hands up the back of his shirt, pressing her forearms against him, skin-to-skin, he'd almost lost control. Okay, he had lost control a little. Giving her an orgasm in her hallway hadn't been part of his original plan.

The rest of it? He'd been planning what he'd do to her if she took him home pretty much since the moment they'd started talking.

He ran his hand down her arm, then grasped her small breast through her shirt. Her nipple was hard and tight. He flicked his thumb over it and she gasped. Later on, he'd spend more time there. For now, he *needed* to fuck her.

He shifted his hand to her core, cupping its heat and wetness. His dick jerked, radiating waves of pleasure so intense, he thought he might come against her leg. He pressed himself harder against her as she moaned beneath him.

Slowly and carefully—fighting every urge that screamed at him to hurry, to drive himself home over and over again right now—he slid a finger deep into her, pressing on her clit with the heel of his hand as he did.

She gasped, her body pressing tight against him as her back tried to arch beneath his weight. He wanted her to come again. When she'd come in the hall, it was almost like a drug, how it had hit his system. He wanted to experience as much of that as she'd give him.

More fingers explored her slickness. He stretched them gently, making sure she was ready for him. He only wanted to give her pleasure—greater pleasure than she'd ever known. The higher she went, the higher he knew he'd go along with her.

There was no friction, no resistance. She was so wet. Her core clenched against his fingers, begging for more. He sped his hand, increased the pressure against her clit, rubbing it as he slid his fingers in and out of her.

"Kyle." His name came out as a groan. "Please."

She was ready, he was sure. But he wanted this first. Again and again and again.

He shifted more of his weight on her, but kept up the movement of his hand. Then he lowered his lips to her neck and started sucking on the spot just below her ear that had had her thrashing against him earlier.

Her hips bucked against him as she gasped, her core tightening, clenching his fingers in rhythmic contractions. He let go of her neck so he could watch her expression.

Her eyes were shut tight, her lower lip caught between her teeth as she let out little grunts that resonated in his chest.

His dick was so hard. He lined himself up, nestled between her thighs, and waited, basking in her orgasm as he kept coaxing it on, slowing his fingers a bit.

The moment she started to relax, he pulled his hand away and drove himself into her.

"Oh God," she screamed, her eyes flicking open.

Her core was tight, still throbbing with aftershocks of the orgasm she was still coming down from. Her stomach rubbed against his as she arced beneath him again. He pressed himself against her, pounding his hips against hers, feeling her clench his dick.

She wrapped her legs around his thighs and pulled against his grip on her wrists. He let her go, but grabbed a handful of hair so he could pull her head to the side and kiss her neck again.

She pulled up his shirt as high as she could get it. The friction of the material took hers up with it. He could feel those tight nipples rubbing against his chest, her soft skin blazing with heat against him. She dragged her fingertips up his back, wrapping her arms around his chest.

Lightning skittered over his skin, through his flesh, into

his bones. She tightened her legs, drawing him deeper into her body, hips moving against his as she matched his powerful thrusts. Then she slid her hands over his back, pushing his jeans and boxer-briefs down even farther to cup his ass and squeeze.

"Moons, Tracey." He yelled her name as the lightning struck everywhere at once.

His dick pulsed as he quickened to a near frenzied pace. Nothing could feel this good. His nerves were hyper-alive everywhere they touched, sending out pleasure in blasts that made his vision blur and go dark at the edges.

She screamed his name just as her body coiled around him, her core squeezing harder. Her head thrashed against the carpet while her entire body throbbed with energy beneath him.

He kept pounding into her, only slowing when the throbbing in her core finally began to fade. She was still clutching his ass with her hands, his thighs with her legs— as if she didn't want to let him leave her body.

He kept his hips pressed tightly to hers as he shifted his arms so he could lift himself up on his elbows. The movement sent more waves of pleasure through him— muted and gentler, yet still intense. She shivered, but didn't let him go.

Her eyes were shut tight and she was frowning.

He'd thought she'd been ready, but what if he was wrong? He'd never let himself go that much with anyone before while having sex, never felt such a strong connection. If he'd ruined that…

"Are you okay?" he asked.

"Yeah."

"I don't believe you."

"Why 'moons'?"

"What?"

"You yelled out 'moons'."

"It's just an expression we use in my family," he said. "We're all astronomy geeks."

"Great." She still hadn't opened her eyes.

"Would you please look at me?" he asked.

She shook her head. A quick jerk from side to side. "I don't want to. If I open my eyes, you won't be there and I'll realize this has all been a dream."

A tremor ran through him as his body actually shook with relief. He lowered his head to the floor and let out a breath.

"That scared the crap out of me," he said.

"I'm still scared."

He rose up above her again, wanting to see her face, and another of those shivers coursed through her. Her eyes were still shut.

"Tracey…"

"If I open my eyes, and you *are* there, what if this is just a one-night stand for you? Or worse, what if it isn't, but we don't live up to each other's expectations and things don't work out?"

Goosebumps rose along his chest at her words. Not the part about things not working out, but that she wanted this to be more than a single encounter.

"It isn't and we will. At least, we can try."

Slowly, she opened one eye, then the other.

"Still here." He smiled, hoping to ease her nerves.

"Yeah. I am very aware."

Her breath hitched, and he felt her core squeeze his dick. He fought to stifle a groan.

"So… What's next?" she said.

He looked over at the near full box of condoms, then back to her with a raised brow.

A huge smile spread across her face. Her eyes crinkled at the corners even.

She laughed and said, "And then pancakes."

"Absolutely."

Chapter Four

Tracey woke up tangled in the sheets of her bed, feeling sore and relaxed and oh-so-happy with her life choices. Pancakes hadn't happened during the remainder of the night. She couldn't care less.

Kyle was stretched out behind her, one arm splayed above his head and the other draped across his chest. She carefully rolled over so she could watch him sleep without waking him.

His eyelashes were thick and dark. So were his sideburns. She'd expected him to look relaxed and cute as he slept, but there were creases between his eyebrows. His chest rose and fell steadily, but his breaths were shallow and his skin was paler than she'd remembered.

For a moment, she wondered if he was having one of the allergic reactions he'd talked about last night, but then he said, "Good morning."

"Hi. I mean, good morning."

He smiled, and some of the unease left her. There hadn't been too many times when she'd woken up next to someone. Usually, she went to their place or sent them home after a little bit of fun. Last night had been *a whole lot* of fun. Hours and hours of fun. She wondered when the awkwardness of "the morning after" would set in.

She looked over at the clock to see how long they'd slept in. Past noon. Thankfully, it was the weekend.

Kyle stretched, then winced.

"You okay?" she said.

He smiled again, and this time opened his bright green eyes to stare up at her. "Yeah, I'm fine. Just a little tired."

"Did I wear you out last night?"

"I wouldn't say that."

His smile turned playful as he sat up and caught her lips with his. He kept his momentum going, rolling her onto her back and laying on top of her as his tongue delved into her mouth. She wrapped her leg around his thigh to encourage him as he ran his hand along her side and down past her ass, rocking against her.

How many condoms did they have left? She wasn't sure she cared.

That had never happened before, either. Kyle was full of firsts for her. It was terrifying and exhilarating all at once.

Feeling his dick slide against her inner thigh, hard and ready… It was tempting to just shift her hips a little and let him line up to drive back into her again.

But then he stopped, dropping his head to the side of her neck and letting out a sigh. She couldn't tell if it was one of frustration or contentment.

"I owe you pancakes," he said, with one last long stroke against her.

"Pancakes can wait."

She felt him laugh, a rumbling vibration that travelled all through her body. Last night, he'd moaned or gasped or plowed into her faster every time she touched him. She wrapped her arms around him, gently brushing his skin with her forearms as she trailed her fingers along the sides of his spine.

He sucked in a breath, but then lifted himself up, grabbing her arms and pinning them above her head again with both wrists held in one strong hand. The angle put more pressure on her clit where his hips pressed against hers, and she started wriggling against him. He groaned, pushing his hips harder against hers until she stopped.

"Pancakes first," he said. "Or we'll stay in bed until we starve."

"Fine." Was she pouting? She felt like she was pouting. She never pouted.

Kyle leaned down and kissed her again—a light, playful kiss. Then he rolled away from her. He listed to the side as soon as he stood, spreading his arms to right himself.

Tracey rose so she was kneeling on the bed, not that she'd be able to actually catch him if he fell, with how big he was. "You sure you're okay?"

"I'm fine." He turned and smiled at her. "You just have a profound effect on me."

Part of her thrilled at the compliment. Most of her started to worry. The ashen color of his skin was turning a little green. Maybe he was coming down with the flu.

He started to dress, pulling on his pants and shirt, then sat down heavily on the bed.

"You are not fine," she said. She hopped out of bed and grabbed her own clothes, pulling them on as quickly as she could.

Tracey had an aunt who was diabetic. He was almost acting like she did when her blood sugar levels became too low.

"I'm…" He shook his head, then suddenly stiffened. "What time is it?"

"Twelve-thirty," Tracey said.

"Shit." He leapt up from the bed, staggering toward the door.

"What is it?"

"My allergy shot. I'm supposed to take it every morning at eight."

"You're only a few hours late," she said. "Is it really that big a deal?"

She followed him as he stumbled down the hall, wanting to reach out to him. He kept falling against the wall. She'd be flattened if she came too close.

"I tried to not take it a few times when I was a kid. I always became sicker than I've ever been and caved within two hours."

It had been twice that long since he was supposed to take it. What was going to happen to him?

He dropped to his knees by his messenger bag. The contents were still scattered across the floor from when they'd arrived.

"Where is it?" He started rifling through the pile of stuff.

A bit of the clear plastic was sticking out from the side opposite him. "Under the notebook."

He let out a sigh, then brushed the notebooks out of the way. She knew something was wrong before he even reached for it. His back stiffened and his chest stilled as if he was holding his breath.

He picked up the injector and held it up. "It's already been deployed. It must have happened when I dumped everything out last night."

"I'm so sorry."

He shook his head, the movement making him unsteady so that he had to reach out and catch himself with one hand braced against the floor. "It's not your fault."

"I'll call an ambulance."

"That won't help. Carol—my mom—is a geneticist. She makes this formula especially for me."

"You call your mom by her first name?"

"Priorities," he ground out.

"Right, sorry." She pushed away her panic.

This was just like the time she'd had to take Sally to the ER during High School when she'd sprained her ankle during volleyball practice. Or that time Paul had hit Jamie in the head with that baseball bat—accidentally, of course.

Tracey took a deep breath and forced herself to calm down. She'd deal with the emotional aftermath later.

"There has to be something we can do," she said.

"I have more at my place. It isn't far."

"I'll drive you."

Her purse was on the floor near Kyle's bag. She took a step to pick it up, but he caught her arm.

"This isn't how I wanted our first date to end," he said.

"Who said it's over?" She smiled, hoping it masked some of the panic she was feeling, then quickly kissed him. Pulling on his hand, she helped him to his feet. "Come on. You still owe me pancakes."

Chapter Five

Kyle's body was on fire. His skin crawled, his mouth itched, his throat was raw. His eyes burned from the light pouring in through the windows of the car and his ears felt plugged from all the sounds surrounding him. Tires on the pavement, displaced air from traffic, the clanging, clamoring sounds of the city.

But he was with Tracey. He couldn't believe how much that comforted him already in the short time since they'd met.

"You still with me?" she asked, for the dozenth time.

"Yeah."

He kept his eyes clenched shut and tried not to barf. Barfing on their first date was not okay. It was bad enough he was curled in a ball in the passenger's seat, trying to make his stupid muscles stop cramping.

"Come on, come on…" She honked her horn again. The sound reverberated through his skull. His brain felt like it was turning to mush.

"Could you not use the horn? It's too loud."

"Sorry."

He felt the car swerve, his stomach lurching with the movement. Someone else honked, the sound equally painful.

"Maybe we should call an ambulance so they can take you to your place," she said. "Sirens would help cut through this fucking traffic."

"Such language." His teeth clacked as he spoke, and he realized he was shivering. "You k-k-kiss your Grandma with that mouth?"

"My Grandma's the one who taught me to swear. Shit. I'm going to try the side streets. It's longer, but there's less traffic."

He felt the car swerve again, then the sound of rushing wind around him lessened. He let out a sigh at the one-less-stimulus and said, "I think I want a first date do-over."

"Are you kidding? Emergency aside, this is still the best date I've ever had."

A rush of not-pain flooded through him, dulling the alerts his body was sending to his brain. "Me, too."

She let out a snort. "Right. Your date with the nerdgirl —"

He didn't let her finish. "Nerdy girls are the best girls."

"You are not allowed to die. Because I am *so* keeping you."

There was a breathy quality to her voice, as if she'd been trying to whisper the second part of her statement. He heard it loud and clear, though, even over the cacophony on the street.

Another rush of not-pain hit him. Goosebumps tore across his flesh, more intense even than when she'd touched him earlier. His dick hardened, his muscles swelled, his brain felt like it was about to explode.

His ears started buzzing. The only sound that was louder was the pounding of his heart.

Thud-thud. Thud-thud. Thud-thud. Thud-thud-thud. Thud-thud-thud.

Three beats?

Panic surged through him, electrifying his system further. He had to get out of the car, had to get away. What the hell was happening to him?

He reached for the handle of the door and pushed it open. Tires screeched and the car lurched to a stop just as he stumbled out onto the street.

"Kyle, what are you doing?"

He didn't know. He just needed space. Openness. Air.

He opened his eyes to see a kaleidoscope of color. The sky rippled with moisture patterns he…wasn't sure how he could sense. He reached his hand up to touch a particularly dense patch, his skin tingling as the moisture clung to it.

As he watched, his skin turned from a weird ashen-gray to a deep olive green with darker mottled patches here and there. He extended his fingers. Slight translucent webbing spread between them.

"Look out!"

Tracey's scream brought him back to his surroundings. He felt a displacement in the air, sensed the humidity patterns changing as something barreled toward him, and then he leapt out of the way.

The ground pulled away so fast and far. His vision filled with cars and sidewalk and blinding panic. He flailed his arms and legs, reaching for anything that would stop his descent as he started to fall.

Something caught. His hands and feet were on a rough surface, clinging to it. He looked around and saw that he was on the side of a brick building.

Twenty feet off the ground.

"Kyle?"

He looked in the direction of Tracey's voice. She was standing in the street next to her car, her mouth hanging open and her eyes wide.

He needed to get to her and let her know everything was okay. If only he could convince *himself* first. And figure out how to let go of the wall…

Suddenly, his hands and feet stopped sticking to the bricks. He let out a yelp as he fell to the sidewalk, but he landed on all fours instead of his face. He wasn't sure how he'd managed that—or any of this.

The impact hadn't hurt. In fact, now that he thought about it, he didn't hurt anywhere anymore. No burning throat or eyes. No itching mouth or skin.

He took in a deep breath, then let it out. There were

flowers blooming nearby. He could taste it on the moisture in the air. And Tracey…

She ran over to him, grabbing his arm to help him to his feet. His skin blazed where she touched it, his dick throbbed with need. She taste/smelled amazing.

"Are you okay? That was—"

He swallowed the rest of her sentence in a kiss.

This was heaven. He slid his tongue into her mouth. The heat, the wetness, the smooth texture of her skin sent pulsing shockwaves of pleasure through him. He grabbed her ass, lifting her from the ground so that he could walk them back to one of the cars parked nearby. He pressed her against the door of it, wondering if the hood could take their combined weight.

Her fingers dug into his back—through his shirt, but it still drove him crazy with need. He ground against her, grabbing the edge of her shirt so he could pull it off. She pulled her mouth from his, so he latched onto her neck instead.

"Oh God," she groaned. "Wait, wait. Kyle, stop."

She spoke forcefully enough to cut through the haze of lust driving everything else from his mind. He leaned back to look into her face, seeing how her eyes widened as she looked at him.

What is she seeing?

His skin… His skin had changed. And his hands. He was some kind of monster. Some *thing*.

"I'm sorry." He released her, letting her slide to her feet. "I shouldn't have—"

He looked at his arms again. Even the texture of his skin had changed. All the fine hairs were gone, and it was smoother. Not like scales, but something else.

What the hell am I?

"Come back to the car," she said.

He couldn't believe she still wanted to be near him. Maybe she just felt obligated to help. He hated the thought, but at the same time, he didn't know who else to turn to.

They quickly crossed back to the car. Thankfully, the truck that had almost run him over had kept going and no one else was around on the quieter side street.

Once they were back in the car, they both stared out the front windshield. He didn't know what to say. Tracey broke the silence.

"So, last night, when you said you reacted to Earth like a Martian…"

"I'm not a Martian." His stomach—if he *had* a stomach —lurched. "Shit. Maybe I am a Martian."

"You don't know?"

He turned to look at her, once again catching how her eyes widened, pupils dilating. What did he look like now? He could check himself out in the mirror on the back of the sun visor, but…he was afraid to.

"I have no idea what's going on," he said.

He couldn't believe she wasn't freaking out. *He* was

freaking out.

"Are you okay?" Her voice was even and level, like someone trained in triaging situations. "You look like you're feeling better."

He did feel better. The fact that she'd noticed—that she actually cared—triggered another flood of warmth all over his body. He was used to feeling emotions mostly centered in his chest—there was a reason people associated emotions with the heart, after all. This was different. It was like he felt everything all over—on his skin.

"Yeah," he said. "I feel… I feel great, actually. I've never felt better."

"You said your mom is a geneticist, right?"

"Yeah."

"Any chance she's some kind of *mad-scientist* geneticist?"

"No way."

He thought about the incredibly plain and normal childhood he'd experienced in their suburban home. Their upscale suburban home. On a huge plot of land, far away from anyone else. Where Carol worked from home…in a lab…in the basement.

"Oh…"

"What 'oh'?" Tracey asked.

"I think I need to talk to Carol."

"I *know* you need to talk to Carol." Tracey put the car in gear and drove back down the street. "Where does she live?"

"You don't have to take me. I mean, you didn't sign up for this."

"Are you kidding?" She grinned over at him. "A great Sci-fi plot like this—I want to see what happens next."

Chapter Six

They drove up a long driveway flanked by trees that grew thick enough to block out the yard behind them. When the house finally came into view, Tracey was surprised at how normal it looked.

Gorgeous, yes, with the entire front wall of the building made up of windows, and a sloping roof that rose two stories in the front to let in tons of light, then angled sharply to nearly reach the ground in the back. But there were no lightning rods on the roofline, no weird dog-things guarding the door, and no spaceships on the immaculate front lawn.

"Weird," she said.

"After everything that's happened this morning, you think the house is weird?"

"No, it looks normal. And that's weird."

"At least I'll blend in with the lawn," Kyle muttered.

"Well, you know what they say about being green."

"That it's good for the planet?"

"I was going for..."

His lips quirked up on one side in a sardonic smile. He

was probably messing with her, which was great. With what he was going through, he needed some levity. They both did.

The skin on his arms had settled into a deep olive green, with mottled patches of dark brown here and there. His face and the front of his neck was a lighter color—almost yellow.

His features were the same. Chiseled jaw, sensual lips, strong nose, broad shoulders… His eyes were still that unnaturally vibrant green. As she mentally listed her favorite of his physical traits, the color of his eyes brightened, almost as if they were starting to glow.

"Tracey, whatever you're thinking, you need to stop."

She must have been more obvious than she'd thought in ogling him. Now that they were here, though…

She leaned a little closer, resting her hand on his thigh. "Why?"

"Because I don't want to have sex with you in the car in front of my house."

"The back seat is pretty spacious. Or we could run into the woods. We didn't pass any other houses for miles." She let her palm smooth over the lines of his muscle, feeling them flex beneath the thin fabric of his pants.

He sucked in a breath, grabbing her wrist. He entwined their fingers, then pressed a quick kiss to her knuckles before pulling her hand close to his heart.

The gesture was so sweet, so unexpected, even after

everything they'd talked about the night before. Her heart felt like it was in a sudden freefall—not dropping through her stomach, but somehow outside of gravity. The only pull it felt was toward him.

"Carol is in there," he said. "And she might come out here."

It took Tracey a moment to process what he was saying. She shifted her attention away from her pounding heart and focused on their current situation.

"Right," she said. "That would be awkward."

"Beyond awkward. I've never brought anyone home with me before. That plus this," he gestured toward his chest with his free hand, "and I'm already kind of pushing the limits of what my psyche can handle."

"I can wait in the car."

"What about seeing what happens next?"

"You can fill me in later."

He arched an eyebrow at her.

"Wow, that sounded dirty," she said.

He laughed, then kissed her hand again. Her stomach joined her heart in its fluttery dance.

She cleared her throat, and said, "It's more important to me that you're comfortable. And bringing someone home to meet your mom for the first time, that's a big deal."

"I wish the circumstances were different."

"Well, you know what they say. 'Some have green-ness thrust upon them…'"

Both eyebrows went up that time.

"Why does everything I say sound so dirty right now?" she said.

He leaned over and kissed her cheek. Her skin tingled and she could feel a huge, dopey grin on her face, no matter how hard she tried to play it cool.

"Later," he said. "Right now… I'd really like for you to meet my mom."

Her 'one-night-stand' had given her one of the best conversations of her life, followed it up with the absolute best sex of her life, and then turned green and started sticking to walls, but this—*this*—felt like an absolute revelation.

"Are you sure?" she said.

"Yeah."

Her smile must have doubled. She turned toward the door so he wouldn't see just how bad she had it for him. Hopefully, by the time they reached the door, she'd be able to regain some composure.

"Okay." She pulled her hand away so she could grab her purse.

Before she could open the door, Kyle was there doing it for her. When she stood, his arms were caging her in—not that she minded at all.

She'd never been drawn to beefy guys, but being next to him, having him close, she felt a thrill shoot down her spine. He'd enveloped her last night. Taken her to heights she'd never dreamed of, physically, emotionally, and intellectually. He was the whole package.

The whole green package.

"How did you get here so fast?" she said.

He shrugged. "I jumped over the car."

"What?" The word tumbled out, along with a tight laugh. She realized she was tucking the same lock of hair behind her ear—even though it hadn't fallen forward again—and forced her hands to still.

"If I have to deal with the drawbacks of…whatever this is, I might as well enjoy the perks," he said.

"That makes sense."

"One of them is a heightened sense of smell." He leaned in closer, eyes heavy-lidded and glowing faintly.

"Is that a drawback or a perk? I didn't get a chance to shower this morning."

"You smell amazing. Especially when you're thinking about what you were earlier."

"And here I thought it was written all over my face."

"It was written all over your scent."

"I have mixed feelings about that."

"I don't."

He captured her lips with his, moving faster than she could register. His hands wrapped around her waist, pulling her tight against his chest. He deepened the kiss, letting out a moan as her tongue twined with his.

She could feel his dick pressing against her stomach.

Damn, she should jump up and wrap her legs around his waist. Before she could, he thrust his thigh between her legs, sliding one hand to her ass to keep her pinned.

Her fingers dug into his back as he rubbed his leg against her pussy, squeezing her flesh. Sweat trickled down her neck as the summer day seemed to crank about a hundred degrees. Kyle let go of her mouth and ran his tongue along the spot.

He shuddered, and said, "Moons, you taste so good."

"Moons?" she gasped, surprised that she was still capable of speech with what he was doing to her. She vaguely remembered him mentioning his family's weird astronomy 'swears' the night before.

"I know it's weird. I picked it up from Carol."

Carol. His mom. Who was in the house. Possibly watching them through those huge windows that made up the front of the place.

As if summoned by the mention of her name, a woman's voice rang out over the yard. "Kyle?"

He froze, his body stiffening in a much less enjoyable way.

"Busted," Tracey breathed.

Chapter Seven

This was not the way Kyle wanted to introduce Tracey to Carol. He let out a sigh and looked over at the door. Carol's eyes widened when she saw his face, but she gave him a forced smile before stepping further onto the porch.

"Are you all right, Miss?" she asked.

"Oh yeah." Tracey grinned up at him. "Better than all right."

"Carol, this is…" Kyle's voice trailed off as he thought about Carol's question. "Wait, why wouldn't Tracey be all right?"

Carol shifted her weight from one foot to another. "From the looks of things, you're probably dealing with strange urges. I just want you to know that you're stronger than your instincts. I believe in you."

'Stronger than my instincts'? What the hell does that mean?

His hands were sticking to Tracey's clothes, like they'd stuck to that building earlier. He didn't have an excuse for the rest of his body. Seeing Carol standing on the front porch, staring at him as if she was about to start crying, helped him finally force himself to get some distance between them.

He backed away from Tracey. Beautiful, intelligent, funny, delicious Tracey.

He shook his head, trying to clear some of the fog from his thoughts. What had he been doing, making out in the front yard like some hormone-crazed kid?

"There you go," Carol said. "I know you can do it. Just…a little farther, please."

"I think he needs a minute," Tracey said. "Or a cold shower. You know how it is."

She smiled at him, waggling her eyebrows.

"I am going to die of embarrassment," Kyle muttered.

Tracey laughed. "Come on. She gave birth to you. She knows what's what. Unless she grew you in a petri dish or something."

"That's ridiculous," Carol said. "Why would you think such a thing?"

Tracey stared at Carol for a moment, then at Kyle, then back again. "Your mom is *terrible* at bluffing."

"That's not what I meant," Carol said. "The logistics alone would preclude—"

"Mom," Kyle snapped.

Carol immediately quieted. He only used that "outdated relational title" when he was really upset, and she knew it.

He sighed, and said, "That's your first question? Not, 'why are you green'?"

"I…" Carol clenched her lips tightly shut, like she did when he asked questions she didn't want to answer. Like about his dad.

She had known about this all along. She'd known what would happen if he didn't take his "allergy shots". And she'd kept it from him.

The silence stretched on. Tracey looked back and forth between them, then lifted her hand and waved.

"I'm Tracey, by the way."

She was smiling, but her scent had an acrid edge to it. He didn't know what it meant. He was just grateful that it was dampening his reaction to her proximity—and the rich scent of her arousal.

"I'm Dr. Addison."

"I think under the circumstances she can call you Carol."

Carol ignored him. "He's never mentioned you."

Tracey shrugged. "We only met last night."

"Last night?" Carol glared at him. "You've known her for one night, and you bring her here in the middle of a family crisis?"

"Technically, I brought him here—and you guys seem like you could use some help managing your family crisis, *Carol.*" Tracey made sarcastic air quotes around his mom's name. "Besides, I'm not the one who's been lying to him his whole life. Because I'm pretty sure turning green and sticking to walls is not the sign of an allergy."

"I was protecting him." Carol lifted the hand that she'd been keeping behind her back as she took a step forward, pointing it at Tracey to emphasize her words.

Kyle had never seen Carol look so…menacing. The *gun* in her hand heightened the effect.

"Were you going to *shoot* me?" Kyle said.

Carol quickly put the gun behind her back again—as if that would make Kyle un-see it.

"Only if I had to," she said. "And it's a tranquilizer gun."

Kyle snorted. "Thanks. I feel so much better now."

Tracey rested her hand on Kyle's shoulder. "It sounds like you guys have a lot to talk about. Maybe we should do that inside."

"Yeah." He reached up to take Tracey's hand in his, then led her to the porch. When he was standing right next to Carol, he said, "Can I hold her hand, or is that one of the circumstances where you'll have to shoot me?"

Carol opened her mouth, but didn't say anything. She stepped away from the door and let them pass inside.

He led Tracey to the couch and pulled her down next to him. Carol followed, closing the door behind her and locking it. She pressed the button that lowered the shades on the floor to ceiling windows that made up the southern wall of the house.

As soon as the light dimmed, the throbbing behind his eyes lessened. He hadn't even realized he had a headache with all the changes in his body.

"You okay?" Tracey asked.

"Yeah."

Tracey's stomach gurgled. Her eyes widened, and she pressed a hand to her middle. "Sorry. I guess we sort of forgot breakfast."

"I'm the one who's sorry. I was supposed to make you pancakes."

"I'll get you something." Carol crossed the room, heading for the kitchen section of the great room.

She gathered glasses and filled them with water, then rummaged around in the pantry. After a few moments, she walked over to the sitting area. Her metal tray clinked as she set it on the glass-top coffee table.

There were two specimen vials on the tray—non-reactive plastic tubes filled with clear liquid. Sterile swab packs sat next to them.

"You can't be serious," Kyle said. "You want to get a DNA swab *now?*"

She sat across from them with the tranquilizer gun resting in her lap. Her finger was still on the trigger. "Kyle, please, I know this is a lot, but could you humor me?"

"Cool." Tracey leaned forward and picked up one of the swab packs. "How does it work? Do I rub it on my cheek like on TV?"

"You don't have to," Kyle said.

"Actually, she does." Carol's finger twitched on the

trigger. If she wasn't careful, she'd end up firing it by accident. She wasn't quite pointing it at Tracey, but it was closer than he was comfortable with. What was even in that thing?

"It's okay." Tracey tore open the swab and held it up, then stuck it in her mouth. Her words were garbled as she said, "Am I doing it right?"

"Yeah." Kyle picked up the other and did the same, then opened one of the specimen vials. He dropped his swab in the liquid, then put the cap back on and did the same for Tracey's.

"Shake them, please," Carol said.

Kyle did as he was told, holding up both vials. The liquid in Tracey's stayed clear. The one in his turned bright green.

That had never happened before. He set the vials on the table, then ran his hand over his forehead.

"When my DNA sample would turn yellow, you told me that only meant you had to tweak my allergy shot," Kyle said. "What does *this* mean?"

"It means you didn't take your shot on time today," Carol said.

"So this is my fault?"

"No, this is…fate." Carol's lips tightened. "You've always been sensitive to lights and sounds. That will be more pronounced now."

He didn't trust himself to speak without shouting—or

flipping the table. Every word damned her further. How much had she been keeping from him? What other surprises did he have to look forward to?

"You're both hungry," she said. "Please, eat."

She set the tranquilizer gun on the table in front of her, then gestured toward the granola bars she'd brought over. There was also a large glass jar full of applesauce.

"I guess that means I passed inspection," Tracey said.

She glanced at Kyle, then leaned forward and grabbed a couple of bars. She offered one to him, but he shook his head.

"The applesauce is for Kyle," Carol said.

Tracey's mouth was full of food already. She must have been starving.

She covered her mouth, and said, "No spoon?"

Carol shook her head. "His father used to just drink it straight from the bottle. It's a trait they share."

The skin on Kyle's back broke out in gooseflesh, like it was trying to crawl away. "Present tense? My dad is alive?"

Carol's face paled, but she half-smiled. "I don't know. I hope so."

"You've never talked about him before," Kyle said. "Not once. Even when I begged you to."

"It was—"

"Too painful. Yeah, I remember." He remembered all the excuses, all of the fights. He'd never wanted to yell or throw things before, though. He would have written it off as stress due to the fact that *he had just turned green*, but after Carol talking about "strange new urges", he wasn't so sure.

Tracey reached over and rested her hand on his thigh. She didn't say anything. She didn't have to. Having her close was enough to help him curb his temper.

They'd been together for less than a day, and already he was leaning on her, drawing on her strength. What would it be like a week from now? A month?

What had his parents shared—and lost?

"I'm sorry," he said. "This is a lot."

"Anyone would be overwhelmed." Carol shook her head. "You're handling this better than I'd hoped."

"Handling what? What exactly is happening to me?"

Carol gripped the arm rests of her chair. She took a deep breath, then said, "A man was brought into the ER of the hospital where I worked. Unconscious. Unresponsive. They took a blood sample, and it…surprised them."

"Was it green?" Tracey asked.

Carol stared at her. So did he.

Tracey shrugged. "It's a valid question. I mean, look at you."

"Please go on," he said, looking pointedly at Carol.

"They asked me to come in and look at the sample," she said. "I did, and it was unlike anything I'd seen before. I went to the patient's room, and…"

She shook her head, a small smile teasing her lips as her

eyes grew distant. He'd never seen that look on her face before.

"He was, too."

"Was he green?" Tracey said.

Kyle turned to her. "Seriously?"

"I still say it's a valid question." She squeezed his thigh again and smiled. "Green is my favorite color, by the way."

A laugh burst out of him. He shook his head, then picked up her hand and kissed it. He kept hold of it as he set it back on his leg.

When he turned to Carol, she was smiling. "It was like that for your father and I, too. Sudden and…intense."

"He was the patient," Kyle said.

"Yes. He regained consciousness while I was in the room with him and explained what was going on. I destroyed the samples and helped him escape. He stayed with me for a few days while he healed, but then he had to go."

"Go where?" Kyle asked.

She sucked in a breath, probably to come up with some diversionary topic, like usual. Only this time, she held it.

He pushed. He had to. "Carol, I need to know. What am I? What was—is—he?"

"He's an alien."

Chapter Eight

"I knew it!" Tracey crowed, bouncing in her seat. She brought herself back under control as Kyle and Carol stared at her again. "I mean, that's fascinating. Please continue."

"What more is there to say?" Carol said.

"What more—" Kyle bowed his head, letting out a brief laugh. "You tell me my dad was an alien and expect to leave it at that? After I turn *green?*"

"Green is the way of the future," Tracey said.

Kyle frowned at her. "Not helping."

"Are you sure?"

She hoped her attempts at humor were helping him. They were the only thing keeping her from running screaming from the house or curling up in the corner laughing while she chewed on her hair.

Aliens were real. And she'd slept with one. And she kind of had feelings for him.

More than kind of.

He scoffed again, but his body relaxed a bit next to hers. Yeah. She was helping.

She held up her free hand toward Carol and said, "High

five for alien hookups."

Carol's eyebrows raised up her forehead. Tracey wasn't that surprised to be left hanging.

"No? Okay," she said.

"Ugh, she's my mom," Kyle said.

"Yeah, and I'm your...girlfriend, I guess."

His eyes widened, and a huge smile spread over his face. "After all this?"

"You don't go through shit like this together without forming a lasting bond." She glanced over at Carol. "Oops, sorry. '*Stuff* like this'."

Carol waved it off. "Swearing is the least of my concerns right now."

"I'm guessing your not-so-little greenbean is at the center of your focus." Tracey nudged Kyle with her shoulder.

"Don't even think of making that a pet name for me." Kyle turned back to Carol. "So, *was* my dad green?"

"No." She let out a little laugh. "He actually looked much like you did when you were younger. Before your... growth spurt."

"I will pay you cash money to see those pictures," Tracey said. "Kyle says he was a skinny geek, but I'm having trouble picturing that."

"He was thin and bookish."

"Bookish." Tracey laughed. "I like that."

Kyle gestured toward his chest. "If my dad looked

human, why am I green?"

"I don't know," Carol said. "From what he told me, his species were originally amphibious. Perhaps they had coloration that fits what your body is expressing. He did tell me that their geneticists modified their DNA to change their appearance generations ago."

"So that they could fit in on Earth and invade?" Tracey had read so many books like that.

"No, they did it to fit in with the dominant society," Carol said. "Most of the galaxy is controlled by the Coalition of Planets. The ruling species are from Sadr-4. Their appearance is similar enough to ours that his people speculate Earth might be a lost colony."

"No way." Tracey beamed at Kyle. "I guess that means I'm an alien, too."

"*If* they're correct, I suppose we all are," Carol said.

Tracey dropped her empty wrapper on the tray. "Is that why you wanted to test my DNA, too? To make sure I'm not an alien in disguise?"

"We can't be too careful," Carol said. "Most of the aliens I've heard about aren't very friendly."

"I want to hear all those stories." If Tracey was going to be living a Scifi novel, she wanted to get the most out of it.

"I don't understand how you're handling this so well," Carol said.

"Kyle isn't the only 'bookish' one." Tracey reached into her purse and pulled out the book she and Kyle had bonded over last night.

Carol rolled her eyes. "Now it makes sense that you two bonded so quickly. He loves that series."

"I keep telling you to give them a try," Kyle said. "Although, I guess I understand better what you meant when you kept saying they were too unrealistic."

Carol smiled at him gently. "I know the emotional ramifications of this must be intense, but how are you feeling otherwise?"

"Honestly? I feel great," Kyle said. "Never better."

Carol nodded. "I'm not surprised. I'm glad to hear it, though. Suppressing your DNA on such a large scale hasn't been easy."

"You know what else isn't easy? Being—"

Kyle cut Tracey off before she could finish her amazing joke.

"But you didn't know I'd change this radically," he said.

"Your father looked human for the most part, but he had incredible strength and he could cling to walls." Carol actually laughed a little. "That would have been hard to explain during parent-teacher conferences."

"What parts of him didn't look human?" Tracey asked.

"Again," Kyle said. "My mom."

"I wasn't thinking about that, you perv." Although now that he brought it up, she was kind of curious.

"His teeth." Carol held up her hands as if warding off the topic. "Just his teeth."

"Did he have like shark teeth or something?" Tracey asked.

"No." Carol looked over at Kyle intently, as if wary of his reaction. "He had fangs embedded in the roof of his mouth."

"Fangs?" Tracey reached out for Kyle's lips. "Let me see."

Kyle caught her hands by the wrists, but her momentum made her land against his chest—not that she minded. His pupils dilated as he stared down at her. Dilated sideways, in an oblong pattern.

"Cool…" she said.

"I do not have fangs in the roof of my mouth," he said. "I'd be able to feel them."

"Oh, right."

He helped her sit back up, but this time, put his arm around her shoulders, tucking her against his side. Instead of overheating in the balmy weather, he was actually cool. She could feel her warmth siphoning into him in a pleasant way.

"Your father and I had no idea that his Sadirian DNA would make us biologically compatible enough to produce offspring," Carol said. "If he'd known I was pregnant, I don't think he would have left."

Kyle tensed at Tracey's side. "Then why did he leave?"

"His people may not have altered their appearance with the intention of invading Earth, but they're making use of it now," Carol said.

"Wait, so they *are* invading Earth?" Tracey wondered if she'd ever encountered an alien before and not even realized it. That funky lady at the tea shop seemed a likely candidate.

When Carol didn't respond, Kyle said, "Carol?"

"They're not here to take over the planet," she said.

"Okay…" He drew out the word. "Then why are they here?"

"They're collecting chemicals to improve their quality of life."

"That doesn't sound so bad," Tracey said.

Kyle shook his head. "There's more you're not telling us."

"The chemicals they need are generated by humans." Carol rushed on. "But your father never bit me, even though he could easily have done so."

"Oh my God." Kyle started to pull away, but Tracey gripped his thigh and shifted closer to him.

"They don't kill people," Carol said. "They just siphon off the chemicals they need from the bloodstream."

"Like that makes it better?" he yelled.

"You're my son. You are not a monster."

"Look at me, mom. Look at me and tell me I'm not a monster."

"Come on," Tracey said. "Breathe."

He covered his face with his hands for a few moments,

his huge chest expanding and contracting as he took several deep breaths. Tracey reached over and rubbed his back, keeping her other hand on his knee.

After a few moments, he leaned forward, clasping his hands in front of him. "So, let me get this straight. I am half human, half...vampiric genetically engineered amphibious-human alien?"

"That doesn't change who you are," Carol said.

He snorted.

"She's right," Tracey said. "Just because your dad is a... vampire...space...frog, that doesn't mean he's a monster. Or that you are."

Kyle let out a light laugh. "'Vampire space frog'?"

"It's a lot easier to say than 'vampiric genetically engineered amphibious-human alien."

"You could just call them by their species name," Carol said.

Tracey and Kyle both looked up at her, waiting.

"In the Coalition, they're known as the Tau Ceti."

Chapter Nine

"Can you change me back?" It was the one question at the front of Kyle's mind, and the one he most dreaded getting an answer to.

"I'm not sure," Carol said. "We can try, but the fact that you've changed so much… It was easier to keep the DNA dormant than it will be to force it back into dormancy. The process may be painful."

"That doesn't matter," he said. "We need to reverse this."

"I don't know, I think you look hot." Tracey was still resting her hand on his back.

Carol might think Tracey wasn't freaking out, but he knew better. That acrid edge to her scent had sharpened when Carol was holding the gun, and dulled when she put it on the table. It remained an undercurrent in whatever pheromones Tracey was putting off that Kyle could now detect.

Fear. An undercurrent to the near-constant lust.

He was sure that was the sweet scent that surrounded her —like honey barbeque. He tried to ignore it, along with the effect it was having on his body.

"I can't walk around looking like this," he said.

Tracey shrugged. "We could buy a bunch of foundation and get you some turtlenecks. Although, that might not feel too great with our summers."

"Summer weather has never bothered me." He turned to Carol and said, "Is that a side-effect of all this?"

She nodded. "Probably. Tau Ceti-5 is a swamp planet with high heat and humidity and extensive plant life. The Tau Ceti evolved to suit that environment. That's why your eyes have always been sensitive to light. Your hearing will be amplified as well, if you follow after Alan."

"Alan?" Kyle's stomach lurched. "Is that his name?"

Carol nodded, that same half-smile that Kyle had never seen before today on her face. "His Earth name, anyway. He told me I'd never be able to pronounce the Tau Ceti one."

Kyle snorted. Even with all the changes, there were still things he was grateful for. Learning about his father—and his mother. He'd never seen this side of her.

"Is it a play on the word 'alien'?" Tracey asked.

Carol shook her head. "No, I think it was just the name assigned to him."

"It sounds so…normal," Tracey said. "Alan the alien."

Carol chuckled. "Wait till you meet Craig and Barbara."

"Who are they?" Tracey asked.

"Lyrian smugglers--who also happen to be seven-foot

tall, white-furred, four-armed...'Bigfeet', for lack of a better term. But don't tell them I said that. Some of the ingredients in Kyle's 'allergy shots'," Carol had the decency to use air quotes when she said the words, "were a little hard to come by. I was able to find an Earthling with alien contacts who could get me what I needed."

"Bigfeet?" Tracey said, her eyes wide and staring.

"You've been working with aliens to keep me looking normal?" Kyle felt like his mind was reaching maximum capacity for 'weird'. He shoved the thought of alien Bigfeet aside, focusing on the alien on the couch—*him*.

"I did what I had to do," Carol said. "They never knew what I needed the materials for, and were compensated fairly."

"How do exchanges like that even work?" Tracey was muttering half under her breath again. She suddenly sat up straighter. "Did Alan leave anything behind? Like something to remember him by?"

Kyle perked up at the thought. He'd love to have something tangible to connect him with is dad—aside from his alien DNA.

"He did, actually." Carol rose from her seat. "I'll go get it. If you'll excuse me."

After she'd left the room, Tracey said, "Wow, your mom is really polite. I don't think she likes me very much though."

"It takes her a while to warm up to people."

"How long are we talking?"

"I'm not sure. Now that I think about it, I've never actually seen her warm up to people."

"Great pep talk." Tracey raised both hands in 'thumbs up' gestures. "Excellent work."

"It's not like that. My whole life, she never dated or had people over. I thought she was married to her work—which I was part of. I had no idea what she's been dealing with this whole time."

Tracey put her hand back on his thigh. "Well, now you do. It can help you become closer."

"I know this is affecting you more than you're letting on."

"Pshaw." She lifted her shoulders briefly and looked away, acting like it was no big deal.

"Tracey…"

"Okay, yeah. It's a lot," she said. "But for one thing, it isn't happening to me—even though it's happening to someone I like a lot."

"A lot?"

"Let's stay focused. And as you know I read a lot of books. It helps me kind of identify better with what you're going through."

"So, you're still sticking around for the Scifi plotline, huh?"

"I'm sticking around because you're the hottest, smartest, coolest guy I've ever dated. So you're also a green alien. As far as I'm concerned, that's a bonus."

"You need to add 'luckiest' to your list."

"Yeah, I am pretty great, too." She nodded thoughtfully, then a huge grin spread over her face.

He cupped her cheek, leaning down to kiss her. It was supposed to be a soft, gentle kiss. A reassurance and reminder of what they'd shared. Then again, what they'd shared had been anything but.

As soon as their lips touched, his skin erupted in tingling sensations that soaked into his muscles, his bones. Every part of him cried out for more.

He slid his tongue into her mouth, pushing her back onto the couch and covering her body with his. She was just starting to pull his shirt up when he heard someone clear their throat in the kitchen.

Shit.

Carol. Right.

He broke off the kiss, but held Tracey's gaze for a few moments. There was no levity, no jokes, just the same sense of awe that he felt reflected on his own features. That they had found each other, were facing this together. More than anything else, it made him believe in miracles.

"I can leave this on the counter," Carol said.

Tracey muttered "busted" under her breath before casting a quick grin at him.

"That's okay, we just need a minute." He leaned back, pulling her along to sit next to him.

"Only a minute?" Tracey said. "Give yourself more credit than that."

He sighed and let his head drop forward, shaking his head. "Do you ever take anything seriously?"

"All the time," she said. "But I almost never act like it."

"Humor is an effective coping mechanism for stressful situations." Carol headed toward them carrying a small box. She paused on the other side of the coffee table. "This is yours now."

Kyle took the box and opened it. Inside, there was a small silver triangle with a sphere at its center. He'd seen similar designs for the spaceships in old-school Scifi movies.

"This is it?" Kyle asked.

"It's all he left with me." She smiled, and added, "Besides you."

Tracey wrapped her arm around Kyle's back. He took a moment to just feel her presence.

"Why did he leave?" Kyle said. "If he felt the same way about you that you obviously still feel about him… I don't get it."

Carol sat down across from them again. "He was trying to keep me safe. Earthlings aren't supposed to know that aliens are real. And the Tau Ceti aren't supposed to be here at all. If we'd been discovered, I would have had my memory purged with a mind-wipe, and he'd have been imprisoned—and that's if the Coalition found us."

"What if it had been the Tau Ceti?" he asked.

She shook her head. "I don't know. I can't imagine they would look kindly on deserters, though. And they are a more...violent species, from what Alan told me."

"Great." Kyle gripped the box tighter.

"There are exceptions to every group," Carol said. "Alan was one of them. From what I've seen, you are, too. Have you noticed any changes in your thoughts or emotions?"

Thoughts? Not so much. Emotions... That was another story, especially with Tracey sitting so close, offering support. But that didn't have anything to do with his transformation.

He hoped so, anyway.

He didn't give voice to his concerns. Instead, he shook his head.

Carol smiled. "I didn't know what to expect when your alien DNA asserted itself. The chemical in the tranquilizer wouldn't have harmed you."

"Thanks for that, I guess." He was glad Carol was protecting herself.

He stared at his reflection in the triangle within the box, stretched and warped on the sphere's surface. And very, very green.

"Here." He shoved the box toward Tracey.

"What do you want me to do with it?" she said.

"I don't care. I just...can't."

Tracey looked down at the box. Her lips softened and

she shook her head. Then she lifted the triangle from the box.

"Kyle, it's going to be okay," she said.

"Right. I can become the new spokesman for green energy, or landscaping. And hey, when it comes to hide-and-seek in the summertime, no one will ever find me."

"This is who you are," Tracey said. "And you can't hide from that."

She handed him the triangle. It was cool at first, but warmed quickly in his palm.

Then started to glow.

"Does it always do that?" Tracey asked.

"It's never done that before." Carol stood quickly, leaning over to get a better look.

The glow turned into a pulsing light that was accompanied by a strange trilling sound.

"What about that?" Kyle said.

Carol shook her head.

Tracey let out a short laugh, but the acrid note to her scent had risen again. "At least it's not getting faster and louder, like it's going to detonate or something."

The pulsing grew faster and the sound increased.

"I had to say something," Tracey said.

"Stay here." Kyle stood and leapt across the room to the door that led to the back yard. He overshot his mark and stumbled into the glass, but recovered quickly. He threw the door open and ran outside, heading for the trees.

The trilling sound had become a single sustained note. Drawing back his arm, he threw the triangle as far as he could. He turned back to the house and saw Carol and Tracey standing just outside the door.

"I said to stay inside," he yelled.

"You're not the boss of me," Tracey shouted back. "Now get your green ass back inside."

He leapt across the yard, landing right in front of them, then herded them into the living room.

"We should get to the lab," Carol said.

"No time." He pushed them to the floor, hugging them together with his back toward the wall that separated them from the blast. He clenched his eyes shut and waited.

And waited.

After a few moments, he dared to open his eyes and look over his shoulder. Tracey had her arms over the back of her head. She lowered them, looking first at Carol and then Kyle.

"Well, that was anticlimactic," Tracey said.

Kyle felt the pressure wave punch through his gut right before the ground beneath them rocked as a deafening sound hit the house.

Chapter Ten

Glass shattered everywhere. The sliding door to the back yard, the entire front wall of windows, even the coffee table broke into clear pebbles that rained over the tile floors.

"I'm not allowed to speak ever again." Tracey's ears were ringing from the explosion. She couldn't believe the walls had held. She glanced at the floor, expecting to see hazardous shards everywhere, but everything had broken into smooth pebbles. "You built your house out of safety glass?"

"And reinforced beams," Carol said. "The lab has explosive chemicals in it, so I planned accordingly when I had the place built."

"I had no idea geneticists needed explosive chemicals," Tracey said.

"I'm also storing some things for Barbara."

"Is everyone okay?" Kyle stood, one arm gripping Tracey and the other Carol as he helped them up.

Tracey shook some safety glass out of her hair. "I'm fine."

Carol nodded.

The smell of smoke wafted in from the empty door frame. They walked closer, clustered in their little group.

The grass was blackened. Most of the trees at the edge of the property were lying flat on the ground. For as far as she could see, there was only desolation.

"What the fuck was that?" Tracey asked.

"I had no idea that would happen." Carol's voice was raw. "I've held it before—when I was thinking of Alan and missing him, and that never happened. Why… Why would he leave that with me?" She covered her mouth with her hand and clenched her eyes shut, tears rolling down her cheeks.

Tracey put her arm around Carol's waist and pulled her closer. She didn't care that they'd just met. Pain of that magnitude called for extreme measures.

"Maybe he didn't think it would ever be set off," Tracey said.

"I asked Craig to look at it to see if he could get a message to Alan." Carol looked at Kyle through tear-filled eyes. "I wanted him to know about you. They couldn't figure out what it was or how it worked."

"So Lyrians and humans can touch it," Tracey said. "But not…"

"Not someone with Tau Ceti DNA," Kyle said. "He was trying to protect you from beings like me."

"Not like you," Carol said.

At the same time, Tracey said, "Get over it already."

He glared at her, but she didn't back down. Instead, she stepped closer to his hulking frame, till their chests almost touched.

"You're an alien," she said. "You're green. That's weird and scary. I get it. But I don't think that's what's freaking you out."

"You know me so well after less than a day, please, tell me all about myself." Kyle spoke through gritted teeth.

Our first fight. Great.

Tracey let her momentum carry her along, speaking from her gut—a gut that was trained by growing up with a huge family and having probably hundreds of soul-searching talks with them all.

"From the moment I met you, you've been apologizing for how you look—even before you turned green—and trying to paint a picture of who you want me to think you are. 'I really love books! I haven't always been this beefy.' Trying to make me see you the way you want me to—as if I can't make up my mind for myself."

She planted her hands on her hips. It was that or jab a finger into his chest to emphasize her point.

"I get it now," she said. "You're scared I'm going to leave because you didn't know before why your dad left. And since your mom is Mrs. Protect-o when it comes to you and never talked about it, you've probably always been pretty sure it's your fault. Well, surprise! He didn't leave because he thought you'd turn green or muscly, or be too human or too froggy. He didn't even know about you. So stop trying to think he's right about things he never even thought about."

"What does that even mean?" Kyle said.

"You're not a monster and you're not going to become one just because you're half-alien," she said. "He didn't leave the bomb to protect Carol from you."

Tracey was dimly aware of Carol turning in her periphery and taking a step toward the back door. Kyle's eyes widened as he looked at something over Tracey's shoulder.

"No, he didn't." Kyle swallowed hard, the muscles in his neck standing out briefly. "I think he left it to protect her from them."

Tracey turned to see a ship hovering over the yard. It was only about as big as the house and had a triangular shape that was too reminiscent of the device that had blown up the forest to be a coincidence. Hatches opened in its underside and landing gear popped out as it descended.

"Oh shit," Tracey said. "Who let me talk again?"

"The lab." Carol's gaze was fixed on the ship, but her arms flailed behind her, shoving them deeper into the house. "Get to the lab."

"Go!" Kyle grabbed Carol's arm and pushed her forward.

Tracey didn't wait for more urging. She ran as fast as she could after Carol while also checking to make sure

Kyle was following.

Carol paused at a door with a digital keypad next to it. Her hands were shaking as she pressed the buttons. The door opened, revealing a stairwell. She ran down the steps, skipping some by using the railing to support her rapid descent.

At the bottom, there was another digital lock, along with a handprint scanner and what Tracey thought was a retinal scanner. She turned back to the stairs to see Kyle at the door above them.

"Don't you dare think about going out there yourself." Tracey started back up the stairs, but Kyle quickly slammed the door and headed down toward her.

"I was thinking about grabbing the tranq gun from the living room floor, but there was no way I could get to it in time," he said.

"Fine." She grabbed his hand as soon as he was within reach. "Now let's move."

Carol opened the door, and said, "Come on."

They all stumbled through, then Carol turned and shut the door, keying in something, then backing away from it.

"Weapons," Tracey said. "Do you have any more tranq guns down here?"

Carol shook her head. "No. That was my only one. It also had my only dose of the chemical that incapacitates the Tau Ceti in it."

"Great." Tracey's mind was racing. She looked around

the lab, at the beakers and tables and back-lit cabinets full of who knew what. "Wow, this place is really cool."

"Maybe they won't find us down here," Carol said.

The floor shook, a huge boom sounding from the stairwell.

"No such luck." Tracey kept scanning the room, trying to think of anything that might help, remembering stories she'd read, movies she'd seen.

"We don't have much time," Kyle said. "What about those explosive chemicals? Can we use those?"

"Not without blowing ourselves up as well," Carol said.

"That might be our only option." Tracey paused as the others looked at her. "Come on, Kyle. Think it through. That bomb was activated by Tau Ceti DNA. Carol, you said the Tau Ceti are violent. Your dad might have been trying to protect her from them if she was ever found. A quick exit."

"They can't be that bad," Kyle said. "I thought you said I'm not a monster."

"*You're* not." She gestured toward the door to the stairwell. "I don't know about them. I just know we need to be ready. Carol, can you rig it so we can hit a button or something if it looks like that's our only out?"

Carol nodded. "I think so."

"No," Kyle said. "No way."

"It's only a last resort," Tracey said.

"*I* am the last resort. And I'm not letting anything happen to either of you."

Chapter Eleven

The door started to glow before anyone could argue further. Kyle stared at the ceiling above it.

I really hope this works.

He leapt, visualizing his hands and feet sticking to the smooth surface above them. As soon as his skin made contact, he felt it connecting somehow.

Carol is going to want to run more tests after this.

He managed to crawl across the room to the door, positioning himself so that he could drop down on whoever —or whatever—came through. He held his breath, willing his plan to succeed.

With nowhere to hide, Tracey and Carol were standing at the opposite end of the room. The stern expressions on their faces sent a chill down his spine. They looked ready to take on anything.

A high pitched whine picked up behind the door. The glow was so bright, Kyle had to shut his eyes. He saw a flash even through his eyelids, then the sound and light was gone. When he looked again, the door had vanished.

Three men ran in. They were wearing jeans and T-shirts

with jackets over them and looked absolutely human. More human than Kyle.

The ray guns they were carrying caught his attention even more. The weapons were brass colored, with rings around the pointed barrels that made them look like something straight out of a 50's Scifi movie.

The one in front raised his gun. His jacket had a name badge sewn onto it that said, "John".

"Who set off that ancient beacon?" John said.

Tracey stepped forward way too aggressively. "It's not *that* old."

"Thank you." Carol kept her gaze fixed on the men.

John pointed his gun at one of the worktables and fired. It glowed brightly for a split-second before vanishing. Then he turned back to Carol and Tracey.

"I won't ask again," he said.

"It was me." Tracey raised her hands and took a step forward. "I set it off."

The two men behind the first one laughed.

"What's so funny about that?" Tracey said.

"Shut up." John must be the leader, from the way the other two suddenly stiffened. "No lies. One of our scouts had to have been here to set it off."

"I could be a Tau Ceti scout." Tracey actually sounded offended.

Carol leaned forward and whispered, "All Tau Ceti are male."

"Oh." Tracey gave an exaggerated nod. "No wonder you guys have a reputation for being dicks."

One of the guys in the back actually snickered. John lashed out, smacking his underling in the face with his gun. Bright red blood splattered out of the guy's crushed nose, standing out in livid contrast on the white floor.

It was the perfect distraction. Kyle dropped down on John's back, grabbing at the guy's arms to try to pin them to his sides. They didn't budge. The Tau Ceti was so solid, it felt like Kyle had landed on a rock.

John reached behind him and grabbed Kyle's shoulder, digging his fingers into his flesh. Pain blinded him as his arm went limp. Then Kyle was flying through the air, the far side of the room coming up so fast he barely had time to raise the arm that still had feeling in it to keep from face-planting into the wall. He bounced off the surface, his good arm stinging from the impact, and landed in a heap on the ground.

At least he was closer to Carol and Tracey and could protect them. Except, when he'd recovered enough to look around, they were gone.

There was scuffling and yelling by the door. Kyle looked up just in time to see Carol throw a beaker of something in the face of one of the Tau Ceti. Steam rose from his skin and he screamed. While John lunged for Carol, Tracey dove to the floor. She rolled onto her back, one of the weapons held in her hand. She pointed it at the nearest Tau Ceti, and a beam of bright yellow light shot out of it.

The guy was still yelling from whatever Carol had thrown at him. He glowed for a moment, then disappeared.

"I got one." Tracey's eyes widened. "Oh shit! I just killed someone."

"Tracey," Carol yelled.

Tracey's head jerked up at the sound of Carol's voice. John held Carol in that iron grip against his chest. He was small enough that Carol's body completely blocked him. How the hell was he so strong?

"This one, I need." John lifted his weapon again. "You, not so much."

"Wait!" Kyle yelled.

Everyone paused.

"Tracey, put down your gun," he said.

"But…"

Kyle slowly rose. "Just do it."

He flexed his injured arm as the feeling started to return to it—needles of pain radiating out from his shoulder. Tracey lifted her hands in a gesture of surrender he prayed the aliens understood, then set the gun on the floor next to her. She scooted away from the group, heading closer to Kyle after she stood.

"What is that?" The Tau Ceti with the broken nose stared at him. His bloodstained badge read, "Toby".

"I don't know, but I think this Earthling can tell us,"

John said.

Carol gasped as he tightened his grip.

"Mom." Kyle took a step forward, but stopped as John lifted his weapon.

"Only someone with Tau Ceti DNA could set off that beacon." John glanced from Kyle to Carol and back again. "Would you care to explain, *'Mom'*?"

"Not really," Carol said.

Shit. Kyle shouldn't have let that slip. Now, Carol was in even more danger.

John glanced around. "This place looks like a laboratory. Did you capture a scout and dissect him? Maybe use his DNA to create this abomination?"

"My son is no abomination," Carol said.

Tracey took a step closer to Kyle. "Love is love, asshats."

"Love?" John sniffed the air, then paled, giving a greenish cast to his skin. "You've pair bonded with that thing."

"That's one word for it." Tracey cast a tight smile at Kyle.

He couldn't imagine what she must be going through after killing that Tau Ceti. At the same time, Kyle was certain those aliens wouldn't have a moment's hesitation in killing the rest of them.

"I'm confused," Toby said. "Then how did the throwback happen?"

"Throwback?" Kyle knew he should be focusing on getting them all out of this alive, but couldn't pass up the chance to get some answers.

"Scouts used to be green a couple of centuries ago." Toby flinched as John lifted his ray gun again.

"We aren't here to talk genetics," John said.

Toby gestured to Kyle. "But we are supposed to figure out where this guy came from, right?"

"Well, kids, when a space frog and an Earthling love each other very much…" Tracey let her voice trail off.

"Wait, a scout had sex with an Earth-monkey?" Toby put his hand on his chest just below his throat. It looked kind of like he was about to throw up—if that was where his stomach was located. "That's disgusting."

Tracey shrugged. "Don't knock it till you try it. How do you guys even breed if you're all dudes?"

"Brood males are absorbed into pools that house spawning queens," Toby said.

"Absorbed?" Carol shivered, then lifted her hand to rest on John's arm. "Perhaps you should explore alternatives. Especially those poor 'brood males'."

John's lip curled up and he loosened his grip. "We've studied your reproductive techniques. They're barbaric."

"Actually, they can be quite beautiful," Carol said. "And informative. Being intimate with Kyle's father gave me a chance to study Tau Ceti physiology very closely."

"Carol," Kyle said. "Come on."

She glared at him briefly, then twisted in John's grasp, jamming her thumb into a spot just below his armpit. John let out a high-pitched squeal that made Kyle's eardrums ring.

Tracey was close enough to grab John's weapon. Toby reached for it as well, and managed to get ahold of her arm. She stomped on his foot, hard. He yelled, but didn't let go of the gun.

Carol was only a few steps away when John grabbed her again. Kyle leapt forward, aiming for John's legs instead of his torso. John stumbled, but didn't fall. Kyle grabbed Carol's arm and spun her away from the melee just as John picked up one of the worktables and held it over his head. His arms coiled to throw it, but then another burst of yellow light shined out in the room.

Kyle saw the after-image of John for a moment before the worktable fell to the floor with a crash. Toby and Tracey were standing next to it, absolutely still, both holding the gun, staring at where John had been.

"That wasn't my fault!" Toby yelled.

Tracey slammed her shoulder into Toby's side, right near where Carol had poked John. Toby didn't let out the same screech, but his face paled even further and he fell against the wall, holding his side. It looked like the Tau Ceti equivalent of getting racked in the balls.

She stumbled away from him, then glanced at the weapon in her hand. With a huge smile on her face, she wheeled around and pointed it at him.

"Don't move, space frog," she yelled. "Oh, sorry, Kyle. I didn't mean to be insensitive."

"Focus on him." Kyle stepped up next to her. "And be careful. These guys are incredibly strong."

"I think this one is a regular scout," Carol said. "No cybernetic implants or enhancements."

"Implants?" Tracey said. "You guys are *cyborg* vampire space frogs?"

"Cyborg vampire…" Toby actually laughed. Then he cleared his throat and straightened. "Yeah, I am. So you should totally give up."

Tracey snorted. "Why would we do that?"

The sound of footsteps echoed from the doorway behind him.

Toby started backing toward the door. "Because I'm pretty sure my reinforcements just arrived."

Chapter Twelve

Tracey really didn't want to shoot Toby. She'd already killed one of these guys, but that had been in the middle of a "fighting for their lives" moment. Same thing with John —which had totally been Toby's fault.

This would be cold, intentional, and premeditated.

Plus, Toby at least had a sense of humor. Maybe they could win him over to their side.

"Stop moving." Tracey brandished the gun at him and he froze. "You're bluffing."

"What's 'bluffing'?" Toby said.

"It isn't a bluff." Kyle cocked his head to the side. "I can hear footsteps upstairs."

"How many?" Carol asked.

He shook his head. "I only hear one, but this is all kind of new to me."

"We have this guy as a hostage," Tracey said.

Toby snorted. "They won't care about me. I'm expendable."

"Then help us," Kyle said. "Switch sides."

A flash of hopefulness crossed Toby's face, but then he

frowned. "It doesn't matter what side any of us are on. The galaxy is about to hit an event horizon, and Earth is on the leading edge."

"We're about to be sucked into a black hole?" Tracey said.

"It's an expression." Carol stepped forward. "The closest Earth equivalent would be, 'Things are about to go to Hell in a handbasket'."

"Let's deal with that later," Kyle said. "I'm pretty sure there's only one person upstairs and right now we're pinned in. Toby here might not be useful as a hostage, but he'll be a fine shield."

"You definitely have our instincts," Toby said.

"Shut up and turn around." Kyle stepped forward and grabbed Toby's arm as he turned around, twisting it behind the Tau Ceti's back. Kyle planted his other hand firmly on Toby's shoulder and started pushing him toward the steps.

"Once we're upstairs, I can…" Tracey swallowed past the lump in her throat. "I can take out the guy. I'm pretty sure I'm getting the hang of these things, and my dad takes me to the range every month or so."

"You still keep a go-bag with plenty of supplies in the SUV?" Kyle asked.

Carol nodded. "I do."

"Sounds like we have a plan." Kyle steered Toby up the stairs and Tracey followed, with Carol trailing behind.

The house was quiet. Tracey's own breathing grated

across her ears—accompanied by her thudding heartbeat. Where was the other alien? Could he hear her pounding heart? She kept her ray gun pointed at the floor, not wanting to accidentally fire off a shot with her nerves stretched so thin.

"My keys are on the counter." Carol headed for the kitchen area of the great room.

"Hold on." Kyle paused, cocking his head to the side again as if listening intently.

Tracey looked all around. She didn't see any sign of anyone else—just broken glass and an eerie silence from outside.

Toby snorted. "There are always three of us, no matter what you heard. You're outnumbered. Probably surrounded."

"So, what?" Tracey said. "I already told you, we're not giving up."

"I don't think you should." Toby craned his neck as much as Kyle would let him, looking at her over his shoulder. "I think you should try to fight your way out, and hope that they kill you. It'll be better for you all that way."

"That's cheerful." A shiver went down her spine. Toby actually looked sincere—like he thought he was helping. She heard a faint rustling in the kitchen just as Kyle turned that direction, holding Toby close.

"Get down," Kyle yelled.

A tall, thin man with dark hair and bronze skin jumped

up from behind the counter, a gun in each hand. He fired one at Kyle.

Instead of the *dzzz* noise of the ray gun, it made a soft *pfft*, and there was no glowing light. The tranq gun. Toby slumped in Kyle's grip.

Tracey and the newcomer both lifted their ray guns, hers pointing at him, but his still locked on Kyle. Before either could fire, Carol jumped between them, screaming, "Wait!"

For the second time, everyone froze.

Carol was the first to come unstuck. She took a few hesitant steps toward the new alien, and said, "Alan?"

Kyle let Toby slide to the ground with a thud.

"Alan?" Kyle said.

Tracey lowered her weapon. "Whoa. *That's* your dad?"

"Dad?" Alan said. "Who is who's dad?"

"Put down your weapons," Carol said. "We need to talk."

"We don't have time to talk." Alan ran around the counter, keeping his ray gun trained on Kyle. "When this team doesn't call in, command will send reinforcements. It won't take them long to figure out what happened to my team as well, since I ran a trace on the beacon signal that I left with you before taking them out. We have ten minutes, tops, to get far enough away that they can't track us. My ship is outside, but we have to leave now."

"Okay." Carol turned toward Tracey and Kyle. "Come on."

"Wait a minute," Alan said. "If the female is human, she can come along, but the green one is on his own."

Tracey bristled on Kyle's behalf. "The 'green one' is your son."

"Now I know you're human." Alan chuckled. "Sadirians don't know how to make a joke."

"I'm not joking." Tracey stepped closer to Kyle. Reaching out, she took his hand in hers.

Alan faked a laugh. "Ha ha, that's all very funny. But the Tau Ceti don't breed that way."

"You grafted DNA into your species." Kyle's voice was tight. She couldn't imagine what was going through his head.

"DNA that made us biologically compatible," Carol said.

Alan's smile lasted about another ten seconds. His face went lax in wonder as he stared at Kyle.

This could go a couple of ways—most of them painful and sad. Tracey said a silent prayer that Alan would prove to be a decent guy, and at the very least offer to help them all escape. Hoping for more than that seemed too much to ask for, given what she'd been told about the Tau Ceti.

"My son?" Alan said.

Carol nodded. "*Our* son."

Alan covered his mouth with his hand briefly. When he pulled it away, a huge smile was on his face.

"Our son," he repeated. He dropped the tranq gun and

stepped closer to Carol, wrapping his arms around her and pulling her close before kissing her. Soundly.

Tracey leaned into Kyle's side. "I think your parents are getting back together."

Kyle cleared his throat. "We need to move."

Alan and Carol separated—barely. They stood close, staring into each other's eyes and smiling.

"Catch up later," Tracey said. "For now, let's get the hell out of here."

Alan nodded and grabbed Carol's hand, pulling her toward the front door. Kyle and Tracey ran after them.

When they reached the driveway, Tracey jerked to a halt. She knew she should keep running, but her brain locked up, along with her body, as she saw Alan's ship.

It was something straight out of a 1950's Scifi movie, just like the other had been—a disc-shaped craft resting on three thin metal legs with a ramp descending to the ground coming out of the center of it. Only instead of being shaped like a hubcap, it was triangular, and the metal was bronze instead of silver.

"No way," she whispered. She was about to board an alien spaceship.

"Come on." Kyle pulled her hand, casting a tight-lipped smile at her that looked a lot like the one Alan had sported earlier.

Once they were on the ship, she let herself gape again. Alan and Carol were sitting at a control panel. Alan tapped various buttons, and the ship responded with beeping and flashing lights. The ramp pulled up into the ship and the hatch to the outside closed.

"There are only three chairs," Alan said. "You two will have to share."

Kyle sat and pulled Tracey onto his lap. There were straps on the seat, and he quickly buckled himself in, then wrapped his arms around her.

"Don't worry," he said. "I'll keep you safe."

The floor seemed to lurch up toward them, or maybe gravity was just smooshing her against Kyle's body. Outside, grass and trees and roads sped by so quickly her stomach started to recoil. Then it was just blue sky and clouds for a few seconds, and then…

"Holy shit." Tracey gripped Kyle's hand so tight her fingers started to tingle.

The front window had gone dark—except for hundreds, thousands, of tiny sparkling lights. Stars.

They were in outer space.

Chapter Thirteen

Kyle had never wanted to be an astronaut as a child. He'd wanted to be a dinosaur for a while, which, he supposed, he was kind of closer to achieving. Seeing the stars in front of him, though, astronaut seemed much better.

"This is amazing," he murmured.

Tracey leaned closer. "Yeah. You sure do know how to impress a girl."

He laughed, nuzzling her hair. She ran her fingers along his jaw, then bent down to kiss him. It started as a light brushing of lips, but once he felt that connection, he needed more. He buried one hand in her hair, tilting her face so he could deepen the kiss.

Carol cleared her throat.

Right. They were on an alien spaceship with absolutely no privacy and his parents were right there.

Both of them.

"I can see where he takes after me," Alan said.

Carol laughed.

"I guess we should probably focus on what's going on," Tracey said.

"Yeah." Kyle looked out at the field of stars. They seemed to be moving past the ship, which meant Alan hadn't stopped after leaving Earth's atmosphere. "Where are you taking us?"

"There's a space station near Centauri-1 where we can sell this ship and maybe find work assignments on one of the dome worlds," Alan said.

Tracey stiffened in Kyle's arms.

"You can't just take us away from our home." There was no way Kyle was letting Tracey be carted off to an alien planet.

Alan spun his chair around so they were facing. "Earth is about to be ground zero for a social revolution. A violent one. We'll all be safer on an obscure dome world."

"I have a family," Tracey said. "I'm not leaving them behind."

"We don't have room for more," Alan said.

"And I'm not taking them to another planet." Tracey shook her head. "Earth is my home, and I'll fight to protect it."

"So will I," Kyle said.

"Even if it means your deaths?" Alan asked.

"Yeah." Tracey and Kyle's voices merged as they answered at once.

Alan sighed. He stared at Kyle for a few long moments. "I don't even know your name."

"It's Kyle." Kyle's voice came out sterner than he'd

anticipated.

He understood that his dad wasn't aware Kyle existed. He really did. But there was still a knot of emotions in Kyle's gut that he didn't know how to sort through.

"Kyle." Alan smiled, and the knot loosened a little. "I want to hear everything. I want to know how this happened —how *you* happened. But you have to know by now that there's no place for you on Earth, or Tau Ceti. Either species will dissect you."

"Actually, he's appeared human for his entire life," Carol said.

Alan's brow furrowed. "What?"

"I created a chemical agent that suppressed his Tau Ceti DNA." Carol glanced at Kyle briefly. "He missed his dose this morning, allowing it to manifest."

"How did you manage that with Earth-based technology?" Alan said.

Carol's eyebrows lifted and her mouth dropped open. She recovered quickly, but Kyle knew that guilty look. It was shocking enough that she'd been working with smugglers of any kind, least of all *alien Bigfeet*. But there was more to it than that.

"You used alien technology to do it, didn't you?" Kyle asked.

Alan rotated his chair toward her. "Carol?"

"I had to do *something*." She gestured to Kyle, and said, "You were born green. Thank God I'd had the foresight to have a trusted friend assist with the home birth in my lab instead of having you at a hospital. And it turned out she had…certain connections."

"What kind of 'connections'?" Alan said.

Carol shrugged with one shoulder. "She's the one who introduced me to the Lyrians."

"Lyrians?" Alan's eyes widened.

She nodded. "They've been operating on Earth for a very long time."

"I don't care about the giant alien Bigfoot," Kyle said. "My priority is getting Tracey safely back to her family— her life. And…" He looked up at her. "I'd like to be part of it."

"I'd like that, too." Tracey smiled. "But I'd also *really* like to meet those Bigfeet. Bigfoots?"

She glanced over at Carol, who pointedly said, "*Lyrians.*"

"Could we ask them for help?" Kyle said.

"We might be able to convince them to trade what you need to help Kyle for the parts of this ship," Alan said. "Especially if they've helped you before. But then we'd be stranded on Earth."

Carol reached over and took his hand in hers. "Is it really that bad?"

"The *Reckoning* is coming," Alan said.

Tracey shifted in Kyle's lap. "That sounds really bad."

"It's just a Coalition ship." Carol rolled her eyes. "They

like to sound important, so they give their ships self-aggrandizing names."

"You really have been talking with Lyrians," Alan said.

"What's the *Reckoning* going to do when it gets here?" Kyle asked.

Alan shrugged. "We don't know. They might arrest everyone who's made contact with Earthlings and try to purge the planet of alien influence. Or, if they think it's too contaminated, they might bring it into the Coalition."

"That doesn't sound too bad," Tracey said.

"And strip it of all resources, turning Earth into yet another world that's incapable of supporting life outside of domes," Alan finished.

Tracey leaned into Kyle's chest harder. "Okay. That sounds bad."

He wrapped his arms around her, and said, "We're not going to let that happen."

"There are only four of us," Alan said. "What do you expect to accomplish?"

Carol suddenly sat straighter in her chair. "We aren't the only ones working toward protecting Earth."

"Okay, now you're talking," Tracey said. "But about who, exactly?"

"The Department of Homeworld Security." Carol beamed. "It's a group of humans and aliens working together to preserve Earth's rights and resources, no matter what happens with the Coalition. And they're based on

Earth." She turned to Alan, and said, "If we join them, Kyle can stay on Earth and still be safe. Or as safe as anyone is in the galaxy nowadays."

"I like the sound of that," Tracey said. "Well, the part about Kyle staying on Earth. The rest of it is kind of terrifying, actually."

"Alan, you can be with us, too," Carol said.

The knot in Kyle's stomach tightened again. He'd dreamed of having his family whole when he was a child, but he'd given up on that long ago. Now, he realized his dream was a hell of a lot more complex than he'd ever imagined. That didn't mean he was ready to walk—or rocket—away from it.

"They won't accept a Tau Ceti," Alan said. "We've had clashes with them already. But they might accept Kyle."

"Alan…" The hope and optimism on Carol's face clouded.

"Turn the ship around," Kyle said. "We're going back. *All* of us. We're going to make this work."

Chapter Fourteen

Aliens, spaceships, her homeworld in danger, and the hottest—and greenest—guy she'd ever hooked up with standing at her side... Tracey felt like one of her favorite books had come to life all around her, equal parts amazing and terrifying. She focused on the amazing part as she looked out the open ramp to the sandy ground below.

"Florida, huh?" Tracey said. "Who knew they were so close."

"This is their newer base." Carol walked up next to her. "Both bases are led by a mated pair of Sadirians and Earthlings, but from what Craig has said, I think we have a better chance of being accepted by this couple."

"Nothing to be nervous about, then." Tracey wiped her sweaty palms against her pants. "They already get the whole alien-human connection, I guess."

"You don't have to do this," Kyle said.

"I know." She stood on her tip-toes and brushed a kiss across his lips. "But I'm going to do it anyway."

She turned toward the ramp and glanced to Carol.

"Ready?" Tracey asked.

Carol nodded. They headed out through the open hatch.

Heat and humidity assailed Tracey's senses. Insects droned. Her feet sank into the soft sand as they walked a few steps away from the ship.

"I think I might prefer the Montana base." Carol swatted at her neck. "If we end up getting to choose."

"I feel you." Tracey looked around at the trees surrounding them. Clumps of silvery moss hung from the branches. Everything was still in the swampy air. She craned her neck around toward the ship, and said, "Are you sure we have the right place?"

"Just give them a minute," Alan said.

Tracey turned back to the forest, and shouted, "We come in peace."

"Tracey…" Kyle hissed.

"It's not working," she murmured. "Take us to your leader!"

The air around them began to shimmer in a dozen places.

"Oh shit," she said. "No more talking, Tracey!"

Carol held up her hands. "Remember, no sudden movements."

Tracey quickly raised her hands. Damn, she really needed to work on the 'no sudden' part of that.

The shimmers coalesced into a dozen small forms. Four-foot tall emerald green lizards surrounded them, standing on their hind legs, long tails whipping around. None of them carried weapons, but a line of metal ran down their backs and encircled their limbs and tails in bands of silver. They had stripes on their skin as well, each in different vibrant colors.

"Oh my God," Tracey said. "You guys are so cute!"

"Tracey…" Carol warned.

"Right, sorry." Tracey cleared her throat. "We come in peace."

"We're looking for the Department of Homeworld Security," Carol said. "We seek sanctuary."

The closest lizard-person-alien-thing cocked its head to the side. The stripes on her side were a rich purple. "What sanctuary do you seek?"

Tracey tried really hard not to squee. They were even cuter when they talked. But they also probably had sharp teeth and would eat her face off if she offended them.

She forced her face into a serious expression. "Two of our group are Tau Ceti. Well, one is a Tau Ceti. Tau Cetian? Anyway, and the other is a human-Tau Ceti hybrid."

A wave of motion flowed across the group, accompanied by hisses and clicks and pops. It sounded more excited than angry.

She hoped.

"Calm yourselves," the first to speak said. She turned back to Tracey and said, "We would see this hybrid. And the other one." She waved her tiny four-fingered hand in a dismissive gesture.

"Kyle," Tracey called. "You can come out now. I think we found your people."

She turned to watch Kyle and his dad walk down the ramp. Alan came first, hands relaxed at his sides. Kyle followed, looking decidedly more anxious.

Another wave of chitters, hisses, and pops sounded among the lizard-people. Several ran toward Kyle, who quickly raised his hands into the air.

The closest lizard to Kyle had stripes the same blue as the water off tropical islands with white sands. She clasped her hands together in front of her, her lips pulling into what looked like a huge smile. In a high, sibilant voice, she said, "He's so cute!"

"Cyan," the purple-striped lizard snapped. "Compose yourself."

Cyan snorted, her tail lashing behind her as if agitated. It calmed when she looked at Kyle again.

"Yeah, Cyan." Tracey pointed at Kyle, and said, "Just so you know, I have dibs."

Cyan kept smiling at Kyle as if she hadn't heard Tracey speak.

"O…kay," Tracey said.

"I was expecting a Sadirian vessel." Alan glanced around at the new aliens surrounding them. "Not…"

"Not a full contingent of combat trained Vegans?" the purple striped lizard said.

Cyan finally turned away from Kyle. "You focus too

much on combat, Violet."

"Vegans?" Alan had paled. "Not… I mean, you couldn't be…"

"The legendary creators of all Coalition technology?" Violet said. "*And* the technology that has been derived from it?"

Alan stammered. "I didn't expect… I mean, we thought you were legend."

"We are not," she hissed. "And it is our new home that you intrude upon, Tau Ceti."

Tracey stepped forward, wanting to defuse what seemed like a volatile situation. "We're just trying to find a way to be safe—well, relatively safe—and help our homeworld. Well, and his family's homeworld." She gestured at Alan. "We thought the Department of Homeworld Security would understand."

"Violet, peace," Cyan said. "These beings seek sanctuary."

"And we will decide whether they receive it," Violet said.

"*You* will decide?" A woman suddenly appeared behind Violet. Out of nowhere.

She looked human, with dark brown hair and eyes, and was wearing a green sundress. The same type of silver bands that the lizard-people wore were visible along her arms, legs, and neck, though.

A man appeared behind her—if "man" could

encapsulate him. "Hulk" would work. Or giant.

He also looked human, aside from pushing seven feet tall and being so muscled, Tracey thought he might be able to pick up their ship and toss it like a football. His thick neck and limbs also sported the silver bands. But he was wearing khaki cargo shorts and a bright Hawaiian patterned T-shirt.

Violet bowed and stepped back. "Only in absence of the Protector. I did not mean to overstep my authority."

"You never do." The woman smiled at Tracey.

"State your mission, Tau Ceti," the huge man said.

"To protect the people we care about." Kyle stepped forward and interlaced his fingers with Tracey's.

She smiled up at him. "And our homeworld."

"Okay, I was talking to the Tau Ceti," the man said. "And you two are not…" He gestured at Kyle, and said, "Well, I don't know what you are."

"He's a hybrid offspring." Carol walked over to Alan and linked her arm in his.

The huge man stared at them for several moments. "I don't really know how to process this."

"Ari, come on," the woman said. "It's obvious. They fell in love, and a miracle happened."

Tracey laughed. "A great big green miracle."

"You know, you can stop pointing out that I'm green any time you want," Kyle said.

"That will not be happening soon." Tracey smiled up at

him. "Just so you know."

"I'm Sarah." The woman stepped forward and extended her hand.

Since Tracey was the one whose right hand was free, she took it and shook it. "I'm Tracey. Garden-variety human. That's Carol, who's the same—except a wicked smart geneticist. The Tau Ceti eye-candy on her arm is Alan, and this gorgeous hybrid is Kyle. *My* Kyle." She glared pointedly at Cyan, who continued to ignore her.

"You can all also stop calling me 'hybrid'," Kyle said.

Tracey leaned forward and whispered, "He only turned green this morning, and he's a little sensitive about it."

"Why sensitive?" Cyan had inched forward and was picking at the hem of Kyle's shirt. "He is the prettiest being with Sadirian DNA I have ever seen."

Tracey stifled a laugh. "Did you hear that? She thinks you're pretty."

Kyle's scowl deepened.

"This is all highly suspect," Ari said. "How do we know it isn't some sort of deception?"

"You don't," Tracey said. "We're asking for a chance to earn your trust."

Kyle put his arm around her shoulders. "We don't want to leave our home. And we don't want it to fall into anyone else's hands—not the Coalition or the Tau Ceti. We're having enough problems taking care of it ourselves."

Ari jerked his head toward Alan. "And you sanction

this? You turn your back on your people?"

"Have you *met* many Tau Ceti?" Alan said.

Ari's face remained as stony as ever. "Fair enough. But what do we do when you begin to crave the chemicals your kind siphons from humans?"

"He won't," Carol said. "He never bit me when we were together. Not once."

"I never wanted to." Alan smiled at her. "Being with Carol makes me happy enough on my own. And that was before I knew we had a family."

Violet made a gagging sound. Tracey tried not to laugh, even though her nerves were pulled so tight that her emotions were all over the place.

So much was riding on this. There was no way she could go back to her mundane life. No way she could leave Kyle.

And if the planet was in that much danger, she wanted to be in the know. She wanted to help.

Sarah looked at the group and nodded, as if coming to some internal decision. "I've seen enough for now. We're going to give them a chance."

Tracey's knees felt weak. She sagged against Kyle's side and let him support her.

"Be advised that my friends here will be watching," Sarah said. "And you can never quite be sure when they're around."

Violet's smile seemed to have a faintly malevolent cast to it. "We will see to your ship and make sure you have appropriate quarters. Our base of operations here is too small to house you, so you will be relocated to Montana."

"Will they accept us, though?" Tracey's stomach knotted up all over again.

Sarah smirked. "They won't risk pissing off the Protector of the Vegans. And I've got a soft spot for happy endings."

Tracey and Sarah stared at each other for a moment before bursting out laughing.

"That sounded so wrong." Kyle shook his head.

Ari let out a groan. "Now there are two of them."

Tracey looked up at Kyle and said, "This was a hell of a first date. I can't wait to see what you do to top it."

"Me? It's your turn to plan the next one." He leaned close and whispered, "Good luck with that."

"Oh crap."

He kissed her, wet and warm and deep, and she didn't even care that they were surrounded by a bunch of aliens or that his parents were…probably averting their eyes and profoundly uncomfortable.

She heard a tittering giggle and another gagging sound and finally broke from the kiss. Looking down, she saw Cyan covering her mouth with her little hands, her green cheeks decidedly rosey. Violet was glaring at them.

Tracey let out a huge laugh at the absurdity of it all. It was hard to believe any of it was real. But it was her new life.

"I think I'm going to love it here," she said.

—

The *Reckoning* is on the way, and things for our friends in the Department of Homeworld Security are getting tense! And they aren't the only ones with problems. Read on for a sneak peek at *Export Duty.*

Export Duty

The Department of Homeworld Security
Book Nine

Chapter One

Lily was heading into a trap. She felt it in her bones as her truck bounced along the uneven gravel and sand that led to the small bungalow at the end of the lane. When she was close to the house, she turned off the engine, but didn't get out of the truck. She needed to plot out contingency plans.

The place looked so innocent. Powder blue stucco—chipped in a few places—and flower boxes in every window, bursting with colorful plants. Palmetto fronds hung above the driveway, as if personally shielding whoever came to this oasis from the oppressive afternoon heat. The house itself was tucked back into a canopy of white pines and oaks.

A bug flew in through the open window. Lily shooed it away.

"Why did she have to build her house on the edge of the Everglades?" Lily mumbled.

A small wisp of a woman stepped out into the shade surrounding her house, her white hair fluffed out around her head like a cloud. Her eyes were as blue as the sky above—just like Lily's.

"Lily? Is that you?" The woman stretched out her arms and made grabby hands. "Come on over here, sweet pea!"

Lily slid from her seat, dragging her purse with her. By the time her feet hit the ground, she was being pulled into a huge hug.

"Nana Lillian," she said. "How are you?"

"I'm just fine." Nana laughed, then pulled back and squeezed Lily's arms. "Let me look at you."

"It's only been a month."

"I used to see you every week."

Lily pushed down a huge pang of guilt. Tried to, anyway.

"I know," she said. "Things at the warehouse have been so busy. Helping mom has taken up—"

"Quit fussing, I didn't mean anything by it." Nana waved a hand at Lily, then hooked her arm into Lily's elbow and headed for the house. "You take things so seriously. I just wanted you to know I missed you, that's all. I have plenty of company out here."

As if summoned by her words, a glaring of cats raced out from the house's open door.

Drat.

The cat treats Lily had brought along for them were still in the glove box. She'd get them later.

Lily was pretty sure she'd learned every word for a group of cats since Nana retired. Clowder, clutter, pounce, glaring. Nana's house seemed to spawn the things.

Meows and purrs greeted them as the cats wove around their feet. Lily nearly tripped a few times, but Nana kept her upright.

"You're not doing your yoga, I see," Nana said. "Skipping your practice isn't good for your balance—on many levels."

"For someone who isn't trying to guilt me, you sure are hitting my weak spots."

"Oh, honey." Nana leaned into Lily's side. "You know I'm here to help. Just...*way* out here." She moved her free hand in an arc, accenting her words. "Do you like living in the old loft?"

"I do. But you didn't have to give it to me."

"Pshaw. I can do what I want with what's mine. And now it's yours."

They stepped into Nana's kitchen, a cooler breeze wafting through the open doorway. Lily wasn't sure how Nana managed to keep her house so cool, but she wasn't about to complain. She really needed to get the AC in the truck fixed.

Nana poured iced tea into two glasses from a sweating jar. She wiped the condensation on her neck when she was done and let out a little sigh, then handed a glass to Lily.

"Let's sit on the back porch," Nana said. There was a gleam in her eye that Lily only saw when Nana was onto a very special find. Treasure hunts, she called them.

Dread curled in Lily's stomach. Was this where the ambush would happen?

Nana had said she wanted to introduce Lily to someone, and wouldn't say more—aside from reassuring Lily that she wasn't trying to hook her up with anyone. A lifetime of experiences pushed back against the promises.

The last time Nana had tried to "introduce" Lily to someone, she'd said, *"You don't have to marry him, just have a little fun!"*

Nana and Lily's mom were both free spirits when it came to…pretty much anything. Lily wished she had half their confidence and spontaneity.

Neither woman shied away from going after what they

wanted, whether it was in the boardroom or the bedroom. Lily was the weirdo who always thought things through and had to have a million contingency plans before venturing into something new.

She followed Nana to the porch, a weird mix of relieved and disappointed to find all four wicker chairs empty. Well, except for the cats.

"Shoo. Shoo." Nana cleared two of the chairs of cats for them. Once they were settled, she said, "Is your mom handling things okay with the business?"

"Of course. Everything's fine."

"Then why are you having to help her so much?"

"I get it. I'll try to make it out here more often." Guilt aside, Lily really did miss their visits.

"Honey, you've got to loosen up a little. Yes, I love spending time with you, but I'm more concerned that you're focusing on the business too much. Is that really what you want to do with your life?"

"How can you even ask? You built that company from nothing. I'm going to take it over eventually, and—"

"Who says you're going to take it over? I built it because it's what I wanted to do. Your mom took over because it's what she wanted. That doesn't mean you have to."

Lily felt her heart skip at the thought. She'd spent her childhood playing among the boxes of rare goods her Nana somehow managed to trade for, buy, or dig up herself. It was like growing up in a museum where Lily could play with the exhibits—as long as they hadn't been sold yet.

But she wanted to make a difference. To help people. She was already brainstorming ideas of how to use the family's contacts and resources for altruistic pursuits when the company passed to her.

"I do want to learn the business," Lily said. "And I'll make it my own when it's time."

"Of that, I have no doubt. But the universe is much more vast and interesting than even I ever imagined. Life on Earth is short, and I want you to enjoy it."

Life on Earth?

That was…weird. Lily wrote it off as something Nana had picked up from one of the books she was constantly reading. They both took big drinks of their tea, then set down their glasses on the wrought iron table between them, moving at the same time. Sharing a look, they laughed at the synchronicity they so often enjoyed when they were together.

Insects droned loudly from the surrounding woods. With the shade of the trees and the porch roof, it was much cooler than the drive out had been. A cat jumped onto Lily's lap, but she immediately evicted it. Even with the shade, she couldn't stand the extra heat it was putting off.

"They miss Cyan." Nana chuckled.

"Who's Cyan?"

"She's who I asked you out here to meet. Actually, she

should have arrived by now." Nana stood and shouted, "Cyan?"

Lily let out a nervous laugh. Cyan must be a new cat. Although, Lily couldn't guess why Nana wanted to arrange a special introduction for this one. Maybe it was super feral, and Nana needed help taming it. Lily was pretty good with animals.

"Cyan!" Nana called again.

"I'm sure she'll come around when she's hungry," Lily said.

"Hungry? Is that a vegan joke?" Nana slapped her thigh. "Oh wait. You don't know where she's from yet."

"Who *does* know where they all come from. I swear these cats are growing on the trees out here."

Nana laughed. "Cyan's not a cat. She's my yoga partner. That's her mat over there."

She pointed at the corner of the living room that was visible from where they were sitting. A couple of yoga mats were rolled up and propped against the wall, including a new one that looked like a child's mat. Maybe somebody with kids had built a house nearby?

Nana would be a great influence on any child's life. Lily really did miss coming out for visits. As much of a pain as it was to make the long drive, the conversations always left Lily with plenty to think about, and doing yoga under the evergreens was an amazing experience.

"We meet out here every day around this time and I give

her lessons," Nana said. "Her tail gets in the way sometimes, but we work around it."

"Her tail?"

Oh no.

The lovely image of Nana mentoring a little girl evaporated in a slew of memories that set Lily's teeth on edge. What the heck was Nana messing with this time?

Once, Nana had saved one of her cats from an anaconda that someone had released into the woods. It had scared Lily within an inch of her life to see the pictures Nana took with the Rangers who came to pick up the snake and relocate it to a nearby sanctuary. The thing was enormous.

Nana had insisted it not be put down. She'd said it was only following its nature. Then she'd found a sanctuary that had an outreach program to teach people about the dangers of introducing invasive species into new ecosystems. The sizeable donation she'd made had no doubt helped their decision to take in another snake.

"Cyan is such a sweetie," Nana said. "You're going to love her. Maybe she's nervous."

"Nana, what is Cyan, exactly?"

"She's a Vegan."

"A 'vaygun'?"

Nana walked a few paces toward the trees, shouting, "It's okay, dear. I just invited my granddaughter to meet you."

"A vaygun?" Lily repeated.

"Yup." Nana laughed. "It's the funniest thing. You remember Sarah over at the Old Oak restaurant?"

"Of course," Lily said.

Sarah wasn't someone Lily would easily forget. She had built her business around a treehouse in a huge oak tree. Sarah lived in the loft at the top of the treehouse, and ran a health food restaurant out of the lower level. There was a deck below, with picnic tables that could easily be moved around for community events and outdoor exercise classes.

Lily had been trying to work up the nerve to ask Sarah for help with the changes Lily wanted to make to her family's business. Sarah had incredible business acumen, and seemed closer in temperament to Lily than Lily's mom and Nana were. Plus, Sarah knew a ton about health and wellness. Lily had already imagined the two of them brainstorming alternatives if a group of people needed medicines that weren't available.

Yeah... Lily really thought things through too much. She needed to work on that.

"Well, Sarah advertised that she was expanding her menu to include vegan options," Nana said. "But she capitalized it on the sign, making it 'Vegan'."

What the heck is a vaygun?

"Okay... So, Cyan is a vegan?" Lily exaggerated the "vee" sound when she said the word.

"No, a Vegan." Nana mimicked Lily's emphasis, but stuck with her mispronunciation.

"I've never heard that word before," Lily said.

"I don't doubt it. There aren't many Vegans running around on Earth yet. But there will be." She gave Lily a quick wink before turning back to the forest.

Lily's nerves pulled tighter. "Nana, what are you talking about?"

"My friend Cyan. She's a little lizard person from the Vega system."

The ground seemed to tilt beneath Lily's feet.

"You're going to love her," Nana went on. "We've been having the best conversations. This world is so new to her, and she's curious about everything. It makes you appreciate things in a way you'd never expect."

Lily's throat was so tight, it was hard to speak. "Nana…"

"She must be invisible," Nana said. She cupped her hands around her mouth. "You can drop your cloaking field, dear. I promise, Lily is a friend."

How suddenly could dementia come on? Nana was in her seventies, but her mind had always been sharp as a tack. She was healthier than most people Lily's age. She took care of herself.

The guilt Lily had been barely fighting off finally won, falling on her in crushing waves. It had been a month since she'd visited. That must have been enough time for Nana to lose her mind.

Nana loved her independence—and living out in the

country. But there was no way Lily could leave her out here by herself anymore.

Lily walked over to the woman she'd idolized for as long as she could remember, and gently rested her hand on Nana's arm.

"Nana, we need to talk."

—

About the Author

USA Today Bestselling author Cassandra Chandler uses her vivid imagination to make the world more interesting, spawning the ideas she turns into her whimsical Science Fiction romcoms and darkly evocative Paranormal and Urban Fantasy Romances. Fast-paced and funny, lighthearted or dark, her stories will introduce you to characters you want to be friends with and worlds where you'd like to build a vacation home.